A Witch Named Hazel

by

Sara Bourgeois

Chapter One

"I didn't even know I had a Great-Uncle Charlie," I said into the phone. I shouldn't have been surprised. You could fill a couple of U-Hauls with the stuff my family didn't talk about.

"Well, Ms. Holloway, you did. You are in fact his sole heir," the man on the phone said and then added, "which does make my job on this case significantly easier."

His name was Joshua Maine and he'd identified himself as my Great-Uncle Charlie Holloway's estate attorney. He also informed that he worked for Maine & Sons Attorneys at Law in a town called Fullmourn. Which I had never heard of before. Neither the law offices nor the town.

"How is that possible?" I asked, but I knew the answer to that even before the question left my lips. My family like to keep secrets, and as I was the black sheep, I wasn't in on many of them. Just the stuff that people got drunk and talked about at the long since abandoned family Christmas gatherings. I wasn't exactly up to date, and apparently Great-Uncle Charlie was never invited to those wonderful, and that's said with a mouthful of sarcasm, family gatherings. "There's plenty of my family left alive, and I'm not the oldest. So, it's not like I could be his sole surviving heir. You must be making a mistake."

"I'm not and you're not, but he named you as his sole heir, so you are," Joshua said flatly. "I need you to come to my office and collect the contents of the estate. When can I expect to see you? It is important this matter be cleared up with the utmost haste."

"What is it?" I asked. "You know, just so I can be prepared. What are the contents of his estate?" *And why is it such a big hurry?* I thought to myself.

Thinking back on it, at some point, I probably should have asked that part. If I had, though, I'm not sure that things would have worked out the way they did. Whether that would have been better, only time would tell.

"We'll discuss that when you come to my office," Joshua said evasively. "Estates are delicate matters, and it's better left to face-to-face interaction. It helps to avoid any miscommunications or misunderstandings. You understand, don't you?"

"It's not like three chickens and a truck full of secondhand furniture, is it? I don't have

3

anywhere to put chickens or even a sofa," I said as I looked around at my cramped, depressing little apartment. As if on cue, the curtain rod I'd just put back up the day before fell halfway off again. I needed more duct tape.

"When can you come to my office?" he asked as he completely ignored my question.

"Where is your office again?" The curtain thing had thoroughly distracted me. Actually, the entire conversation had the same effect. My brain felt like goo. I was.. overwhelmed.

"3752 East Street," he said.

"In Springfield?" I asked. "I don't think we have a street that's just called East Street." This was probably why I didn't make it all the way through community college.

"No, I'm sorry. My office is located in Fullmourn. As was your great-uncle's home and it is where the contents of the estate are located as well. I could have sworn we went over this," he sounded exasperated, and I could relate.

"Fullmourn?" I asked. "Oh, right. You did mention that."

"Do you need directions?" Joshua asked curtly.

"No, I can google it," I said. "When do you have an appointment available?"

"Now," he said and offered no further explanation.

"Well, let me Google it and see how far I'd have to drive. I wasn't expecting this," I said.

"Fullmourn is just under a half hour from Springfield," Joshua said.

"Well, all right then. I suppose I can be there in about a half an hour. I don't have anything pressing going on here this afternoon..." I was explaining when he cut me off.

"Good, I'll see you then," he said and hung up abruptly.

"Busy guy for being a lawyer in a town I've never heard of before," I said to no one but my empty apartment.

It just so happened to be my day off, so it wasn't like I had anywhere else to be at that moment. I didn't have any money to go out, so my plans had been to spend the evening reading while I ate a giant mountain of chicken nuggets.

It might take me all evening, but because of my persistent practice, a high metabolism, and my constant state of low-level anxiety, I could work my way through an entire bag in one night. Thanks to an air fryer I got at a garage sale for five bucks, I could heat them in batches too. Hot, fresh chicken nuggets on demand. It wasn't much, but it was the little things. One of the very few luxuries I could afford with my miniscule paycheck.

"If I go now, then perhaps I can still be back in time for chicken nuggets," I again said to no one. Who was I kidding? I'd stay up all night for chicken nuggets. My work had free coffee, so if I had to drag my butt in there the next day and drown myself in horrible, but free, coffee, it would be worth it. No one would stand between me and my chicken nugget-fueled haunted doll horror movie marathon.

Perhaps I did have plans…

"I told him I'd come right away," I said to myself. "It would be unkind to just not show up." Plus, whoever this Uncle Charlie was, he obviously didn't have anybody. It felt wrong not to show up for him. Even if I had no idea who he was.

I packed my backpack with two bottles of water and a package of trail mix. I wasn't sure how long the meeting with Joshua the lawyer would take, and I really didn't have the money to stop anywhere to eat.

Wendy's had a family pack of spicy chicken nuggets for ten bucks, and I eyed my rent money while biting my bottom lip. Maybe... no. I couldn't risk eviction for chicken nuggets, and my landlord would evict me for being ten bucks short on the rent.

I also threw my book in with my jacket in case I had to wait. Waiting in lines sucked, but I loved waiting somewhere I could just space out or peruse a book. Waiting rooms were great because you had no reason not to veg out and read.

Packed and ready to go, there was nothing to do but leave. I'd lived alone since I was eighteen, so there was no one for me tell goodbye. I locked my door and headed down to the building's parking area. Thankfully, my car was right where I left it. Auto theft wasn't a constant thing in my neighborhood, but it did happen.

After throwing my backpack into the passenger side of the car, I slid in behind the wheel. I punched the address for Joshua's office into my GPS and waited for it to do its thing. My car was pretty old, but it wasn't so old as to not have navigation. The engine didn't always sound like it was going to make it in the winter, but the navigation system hadn't gone out yet.

Chapter Two

You know how as your gas tank gets lower, it seems to head to the dreaded empty faster? A few miles from Fullmourn, I noticed that exact thing was happening to me.

Fortunately, there appeared to be one of those mega gas stations and truck stops at the next exit. I clicked on my blinker and took the exit ramp when it came up.

The sign on the pump looked like it was made just for me.

"Credit, Debit, or Prepay Only."

I had to go in and pay before I could pump because I kept all of my gas money in a little white envelope in my purse. I did the same with my grocery money to make sure I didn't overspend my budget.

After digging around in my bag for a few seconds, I found the envelopes. They were rubber banded together, so I freed the gas envelope and opened it.

There was seven dollars inside of it. That would get me less than three gallons of gas, and it was all I had left until I got paid again.

Obviously, I didn't really have extra trips out of town in my monthly gas budget, but what could I do? I didn't have enough to just turn around and go home, so all I could do was spend the seven bucks and hope that my inheritance included a little cheddar to pad my budget.

I left the car and walked across the lot to the station's convenience store. It was attached to a diner, and there was a sign that directed people around to the side of the building to access the showers.

Since it was the middle of the afternoon, the gas station wasn't too busy. There were only a few cars at the pumps, and it seemed even fewer people were inside milling around looking for the perfect bag of chips and bottle of soda.

I made a beeline for the cash register because I was on a mission. Unfortunately, just as I was about to reach the counter, a man stepped out from behind a rack of gift cards and beat me to the cash register.

"Morning, George," the clerk said. "The usual?"

Oh, good, I thought. *He should be in and out.* I still thought it was rude for him to step in front of me like that, but I decided it wasn't worth saying anything.

Ooh, boy. If a person could be wrong about things, I should have won a prize.

"I won a few bucks on the scratchers from yesterday, so I'll take an extra five today," he said and pulled a scratch-off lottery ticket out of his pocket. The man named George slid it across the counter, and the clerk turned to grab the tickets from the plastic dispenser.

The clerk turned back and slid the new tickets across the counter to George. Thinking the exchange was nearly over, I readied myself to step forward and pay for my gas.

Much to my dismay, George pulled a quarter out of his baggy jeans and began scratching the tickets. If there was a thing I hated, it was people that stood at the counter scratching their tickets. How could anybody think it was okay to just block the line like that?

I let out a heavy sigh, and George seemed oblivious. He just kept scratching.

"Oh, good," he said as he scratched the last one. "Got another winner. Give me five more, Kendra." He handed the clerk the winning ticket.

"Excuse me," I said and cleared my throat. "Can I pay for my gas? I'm kind of in a hurry."

Kendra offered me a sympathetic smile and reached out her hand to take my cash. "What pump, sweetie?"

"Hey, excuse you both," George groused. He turned halfway around and looked at me. "You can wait your turn, young lady. Ain't my problem you didn't give yourself enough time."

I was about to argue with him about how there was no way someone could account for someone standing at the counter scratching off tickets at the gas station when the man who had joined the line behind me spoke up. "Hey, bud. Why don't you move off to the side? People have got places to be."

The man was big, dressed in what I assumed truckers wore, and had the expression of someone who hadn't taken crap from anyone in at least a couple of decades. George sized the guy up and decided the man wasn't someone he wanted to tangle with.

"Fine," he said and moved down the counter a foot. "Nobody has respect for their elders anymore."

"Thank you," I said to the trucker.

He just gave me a nod, and I handed Kendra my seven dollars. "Pump thirteen."

"All that for seven dollars. What a joke," George sniped as Kendra put my cash in the machine and set the pump for me.

"You're all set. Thank you," she said as we both ignored George.

"Thank you," I returned and bolted for the doors.

Chapter Three

The rest of the drive over to Fullmourn was pleasant. The radio played all songs that I liked, and that was rare. Usually it was like one song I liked and a bunch I either didn't care for or totally hated. It was a good thing I had my windows up because I found myself belting out a few tunes. I was sure I looked crazy, but I didn't care.

I was in a decent mood as I drove into town, but I turned the radio down once I crossed over into the Fullmourn town limits. I don't know why but it felt like you could find things better with the radio down. Have you ever tried to read a map with the radio all the way up? Doesn't work.

The navigation took me through the center of town and past the square. I didn't pay too close of attention because I was trying to focus on finding Josh's office, but I did notice there was an old church on one end and several cute little stores. There was also a coffee shop, bakery, and a café. It was a lot of choices for such a small town, but I was impressed. The various eateries caught my attention, but since

I didn't have any money to stop and dine, I just sighed and kept going.

"Maybe on my way out of town, I can spring for a cup of coffee," I told my empty car. "I bet it's good," I said as I thought I caught a whiff of fresh roasted beans. "I can afford one cup."

Just outside of the square was the county courthouse. It was a large, beige stone building with the old jail located across the street. Except I figured out pretty quick that it wasn't really the "old" jail. The building was from 1869 per the stone sign over the entryway, but it looked to be still in use. "Remind me never to get arrested," I said to myself, and then laughed too hard at my own silly joke...

Fullmourn was only a half hour away from my city, but it was in a different county, and it might as well have been in a different world. It felt like I'd stepped back in time, and if not for the modern cars parked along the streets and driving around, I would have believed I had passed through some sort of time portal.

A couple of blocks later, after driving past a diner and a small park, I found the lawyer's office. It was in a former Victorian-style house that had been converted into business space.

He shared the building and parking lot with an accountant and a dentist. The entrance for Josh's office was in the front with the dentist's door being in the back. The accountant's office was on the second floor, and you accessed it by going in through the front door and taking either the stairs or a small elevator up.

I walked past the stairs and elevator to find the door into Josh's office. When I went in, I found myself standing inside a small reception area outfitted with a desk on one side and four chairs around a coffee table on the other. There were plants on every available surface and pots hanging from the ceiling. The smell of lemon-scented Pledge hung in the air, and it quickly became apparent why.

A woman was by the window dusting the baseboards. "Oh, hello," she said and set her can and rag down on the coffee table before standing to greet me. "Sorry I'm not at my desk. I get bored and start cleaning. There is so much wood trim in this place."

"It's okay," I said as she walked around me and went behind the desk. "I'm here to see Josh Maine. I guess I'm his afternoon appointment."

"Hazel Holloway?" she inquired.

"The one and only," I said, but then thought better of it. "You know what, I'm probably not, though."

That elicited a chuckle from the receptionist, who I was about to find out wasn't just the receptionist. "I'm Amanda Maine, Josh's wife and receptionist. I'll let him know you're here."

"Nice to meet you, Amanda," I said.

"It's a pleasure to meet you as well," she replied. "I'm so sorry for your loss."

I briefly thought about correcting her and telling her I didn't know Charlie. So, it wasn't really a loss, but I realized I would sound like a jerk and decided to leave it alone. "Thank you," I said instead.

She picked up the phone on the desk and called Josh. "Your appointment is here," she said before nodding and then hanging up.

"He'll be up in a moment," she said. "Can I get you anything? I was about to grab a cup of coffee or we have Coke?"

I almost said no, but a Coke was a luxury I wasn't about to turn down. I allowed myself one a day at home with dinner, but if she was offering, I was taking. Great-Uncle Charlie had probably paid more than enough in legal fees to cover one free soda.

"I'll have a Coke," I said. "Thank you."

She disappeared through a door behind the desk that I'd assumed was a closet and reappeared a couple of minutes later with a huge steaming mug of coffee in one hand and a bottle of Coke in the other.

"We keep them in the fridge, so it's icy cold. I can get you ice if you want it, though," she offered.

"No, this is great. Thank you," I said.

"You're welcome. Let me know if you need anything," she said and sat down at her desk.

I could only guess that I was in her way as far as her dusting went, so Amanda settled down and began typing away at something on her computer. I sat there and sipped my Coke until Josh appeared at the doorway that led to a hallway and eventually back to his office.

"Come on back," he said and waved for me to follow him.

He didn't wait for me, but instead turned and immediately began the walk back to his office.

Not wanting to lose him, and knowing the house was huge, I jumped up and scurried after him.

"Thanks again," I said and raised the bottle of Coke on my way out.

"You're welcome," Amanda responded.

She started typing again, so I must have well and good ruined her dusting. I followed Josh down the hall and through a door at the very end.

His office was the size of a medium bedroom and may very well have been one when the house was still used as a home.

"Have a seat," Joshua said as he closed the door behind us.

His office smelled like lemon Pledge too. There were a few degrees hanging on the wall behind his desk, but the most notable thing about the room were his framed... napkins?

"I travel a lot to famous restaurants, and sometimes I run into celebrities. I make it a habit to get them to sign a napkin," Josh said as he sat down behind his desk. He must have noticed me ogling them. Probably something he had to explain a lot too. "Now, about the estate."

"Right to business," I said offhand.

"Is there something else you want to discuss?" he said. The way he pinned me with his gaze made me feel dumb.

"No, go ahead," I said. "Do you have to read it out loud or something?"

"You've seen too many movies," he snarked and again made me feel stupid. "I'll just give you a copy, and you can let me know if you have any questions."

At that point, he pulled a manilla envelope out of one of his drawers. He opened it and let a stack of papers slide out onto his desk. A set of keys also fell out and clattered against the mahogany.

"Keys?" I asked as he slid the papers across the desk to me.

"It's all there, but the gist of it is that you've inherited the Holloway and Sons Funeral Home and Crematorium," he said. "The keys are for the house and the hearses. Also, any money he had in his accounts, but he's requested that you keep that money, minus any you absolutely need, set aside to keep paying the mortician his salary."

"I'm sorry," I said and picked up the will. "Did you say a funeral home?"

"Yes. Holloway and Sons Funeral Home and Crematorium," he said again as if it explained everything.

"What about the sons part of that equation?" I was confused. "If there are sons, then why am I inheriting the place?"

"There are no sons. He was one of the sons. The place has been in your family since the 1800s. Okay, well, there is one son. Rook Holloway is the mortician I mentioned earlier. Your great-uncle adopted him, but Rook has no interest in owning or running the funeral home. He just wants to keep working as the mortician. Your great-uncle was happy to oblige, but that's really up to you," Joshua said.

"Can I just... I mean... Can we back this up a little bit?" I was feeling overwhelmed.

"What part of what I've said do you not understand?" It seemed, at least in Joshua Maine's opinion, that I was the dumbest person he'd ever met. I also seemed to be interrupting what had apparently been a perfectly nice day until I arrived. The only problem was that he'd called me. He'd asked me to come to his office right away. I didn't want to be there any more than he wanted me sitting on the other side of his desk.

"Why are you being so smug?" I practically spat at him. I wasn't stupid. I didn't like being made to feel stupid. If anything, I was confused because he was terrible at HIS job.

He looked taken aback. "I'm sorry," Joshua said sheepishly. "I've had a bad day, but that has nothing to do with you. Again, I apologize."

"It's fine," I said and felt bad for snapping. "I'm just not sure what any of this means. It's not like you prepared me for any of this."

"If I had told you what you were inheriting, would you have come?" he asked.

"I…" but I honestly couldn't answer that.

"And that's why I didn't tell you," he said.

"What about Charlie?" I asked. "Will there be a funeral for him?"

"Already done," Joshua said. "Well, there wasn't a real funeral. Ironically, he didn't want one. Your great-uncle was cremated, and there was a small, private service. His ashes are at the funeral home. Rook will have more information for you on that."

"Rook is my cousin, right?" I asked. "My adopted cousin?"

"Your great-uncle adopted him, so I suppose he's some sort of cousin. I'm not exactly sure if he's first or second. I didn't take sociology as one of my electives. Stuck with finance and falling in love with a small-town girl. Now, I've ended up here."

"Is the address for the funeral home in the paperwork?" I asked. "I should get out of your way."

"It is, and so is my number. I know I've been curt today, but I'm here if you have any questions," he said and stood up.

Joshua extended a hand to me which I accepted after I got out of my chair. He was being more polite, but it was obvious he was still ready to be rid of me.

Chapter Four

I pulled into the funeral home's massive driveway and just about died. Pun intended.

At first, I was worried that I was parking my car in the wrong place, but then I realized it was my... house? It was my funeral home, and I could park where I liked.

For a couple of minutes, I just sat in my car staring at the structure. It appeared to be three stories plus a small tower that might have had fourth. If I'd thought the converted Victorian that held Josh's office was big, Holloway and Sons Funeral Home and Crematorium was a behemoth.

Eventually, the front door opened about six inches, and a man with shaggy black curls and a pair of round, black-framed glasses poked his head out.

"You must be Rook," I said to an empty car.

The man offered me a tentative wave, so I waved back. After taking a deep, cleansing breath... well, as cleansing as a breath could be in a car that smelled of dust and gasoline... I could never pump gas without getting some on my hand and thus into the car...I opened my car door and stepped out onto the driveway.

There was a static charge in the air that I hadn't noticed at Josh's office. It almost danced against my skin, and I double-checked the sky for an incoming storm. I'd read that before. I'd seen an article, or maybe it was one of those true scary stories, where someone had felt an electric charge in the air before lightning struck.

A few lazy clouds hung around in the late afternoon sky, but there was no storm front on the horizon. I shook it off and told myself it was just nerves.

I'm not sure that I was ever, or will ever be, able to describe the difference in light in Fullmourn. It was just a little bit darker there. Almost like a mini twilight in the afternoon even though the sun was still up. Lavender-tinged light left strange shadows in your peripheral vision, but it was never enough to make you second-guess your sanity. It was unsettling, but only under the surface.

I'd been so focused on the task at hand that when I arrived in Fullmourn, and even traversing from my car into Josh's office and back again, I hadn't noticed it. Standing there in the middle of the driveway at Holloway and Sons Funeral Home and Crematorium, I noticed it. Still, I explained it away as nerves or my blood sugar being low. What else could it be?

The front door to the funeral home opened wider as I walked up the concrete steps to the porch area. Rook, or who I assumed at the time was my adopted cousin, didn't step outside, though. In fact, he seemed to have disappeared behind the door.

"Are you Rook?" I asked immediately after walking inside.

The interior was exactly what I would have pictured if I'd had time to put any thought into it and yet completely unexpected at the same time. It was probably only shocking because it was far more luxurious than anything I'd ever thought I'd own. Even if it was a funeral home, it was beautifully and lavishly decorated.

The walls to my right and left were both decorated with dark wooden panels, and the walls ahead of me, including the ones that lined the orange wooden staircase, were covered in a gorgeous cream brocade wallpaper.

To my right was a massive stone fireplace, and on the other side was a set of double doors.

"That leads to the viewing area," Rook said as I studied my surroundings. "And yes, I'm Rook."

He didn't extend a hand and in fact seemed to shrink back when I turned my attention to him. I offered him a reassuring smile, but that seemed to make him wilt more.

"Can I go in?" I asked and pointed to the doors. "I mean, is there anybody in there right now?"

"You can go anywhere you want," he said. "It's your place, and no, there's no service in there right now."

"But, is there a... body?"

"Um... we don't usually store them in the viewing room. There might be if there was a service coming up within the next hour, but the next one is tonight. I won't move her upstairs for a couple more hours."

"Oh, there's a funeral tonight?"

"There's supposed to be," Rook said. "I don't think I can act as the funeral director either. I tried to talk myself into it, but I just can't. It's one of the reasons I pushed the lawyer guy to get you here. It's the first funeral since Charlie passed away."

"I'm so sorry," I said.

"Don't be," Rook said curtly, but I could see a bit of hurt in his eyes. Just for a second, and then it was gone. He straightened up and went back to business. "Anyway, I don't think it will be too difficult of a service. No one from the family has come in to pick anything, so I just went with the base package. You'll need to sign off on it and then send it back to whoever paid for the funeral. I think some relative in Kansas. You'll need to look over things. I don't usually get involved in that side of the business."

"No one has been here to plan her service?" I asked.

"I haven't seen anyone other than the deceased. That's my department. The check for the funeral came in the mail with instructions to hold the service today. That was it. My attempts to reach any family members failed, but that might have been because my attempts weren't that great. I'm not usually involved in that aspect of the business," Rook said, and I could swear he blushed. It was an unusual reaction, but I could only guess that he was embarrassed about not being able to, or wanting to, handle the woman's family.

"What was her name?" I asked and Rook looked taken aback.

"Her name?"

"Yes, what was… is her name? So we can stop referring to her as the deceased," I said.

"I prefer not to get too personal," Rook noted.

"I understand," I said. "I would like to know her name. Do you want me to just look it up on the paperwork or something? Is there some sort of rule about saying a deceased's name?"

"No, that's silly," Rook said.

"Well, you're being cagy about it," I retorted.

"I'm sorry," he said and took a step back from me. "This is all just sort of overwhelming for me."

"I understand that," I said. "I feel the same way. But, I need to know her name."

I could tell this made Rook uncomfortable, and it was probably some quirk that Charlie had worked around. I couldn't fathom how, though. How would they speak about the deceased without using their names? Perhaps they just referred to them by the day or time of their funeral. I could do that.

"It's fine," I said. "Where is her paperwork?"

Rook let out an audible sigh of relief. "It's in your office. The physical copies are in the middle of your desk to be signed, and I emailed you copies to your funeral home email address."

"I have a funeral home email address?" I asked.

"I added you to the system. Your password is casket, but you should change that right away," he said.

Suddenly, I realized that I was about to go over paperwork for a woman's funeral, I had a company email address, and I was expected to conduct a service in a few hours. That had not been my intention when I drove over to collect my inheritance.

The plan had been to take a quick look around and then call a real estate agent. I needed to walk the conversation, and the situation, back a few steps before Rook got his hopes up.

"We need to slow this down a little bit," I said. "The funeral home is lovely, but I didn't really have any intentions of staying. I was just going to look around and then call a real estate agent to sell the place. I can't be a funeral director, Rook. I can't stay here in this town."

"Why not?"

That was the million-dollar question.

Because I have an apartment and a job back in the city. It's a crappy apartment and a dead-end job, pun intended, but it's my life.

"You work at the hospital for the medical examiner, right?" Rook asked.

"I do. I'm an autopsy assistant, and the pay is terrible, but it's important work," I said defensively.

"I'm not saying it's not," Rook said. "It's the reason Charlie thought you'd be perfect here. You were going to go to medical school so you could become an ME yourself someday, right?"

"I was," I said. "That's why I got the job as an autopsy assistant in the first place, but since you seem to know everything else about my life, you know I had to drop out of college for a semester. When I tried to go back, I found out I'd lost my admittance to medical school. It was too competitive, and I screwed it up. But I got to keep the job, and it pays well enough for me to get by."

"I think you kept the job, despite the pay, because you know you belong in the death care industry." It was the boldest thing Rook had said since I'd met him minutes ago. He must have been absolutely desperate for me to stay.

"I hate when people call it the death care industry," I said. "What you mean is that I feel called to work with the dead. I can't admit that to many people, but of all the people I know, I'm assuming you understand."

"I do understand, Hazel. That's why I think you should consider staying. You can do far more here than set up for autopsies," Rook said.

"This is going to sound crass, but what does it pay?" I asked.

"It's not crass. I wouldn't expect you to make a life-altering decision without knowing the financials. The issues is that the answer is complicated. We get the fee for the funeral and it varies depending on what the family chooses as far as service level and casket

"I need to figure out moving here. Maybe I should just do this as a trial thing… I really don't know," I said.

"You'll have money to hire someone to move your stuff or at least rent a truck after the funeral tonight. If at some point you decide not to stay, you'll have money to hire someone to move you back," Rook said.

I didn't even have enough gas to get me home and last me until my next paycheck. What choice did I really have?

"I'll do the funeral tonight, but I'm not making any big decisions until after that," I said. "I still might put this place on the market and go back. I'm sorry."

"We'll cross that bridge when we come to it," Rook said.

Before I could say anything else, my stomach growled. "Can you show me to the kitchen? Do we have a kitchen?"

"About that," Rook said.

Chapter Five

"You don't really live like this, do you?" I asked as a surveyed the nearly empty cabinets.

The funeral home had a kitchen. It had two, in fact. There was the main kitchen in the back of the house on the first floor, and the apartment on the third floor had its own.

The kitchen on the first floor would have been a gourmand's dream if it hadn't been completely empty. Well, there were three bags of potato chips in one cabinet and several two-liters of Coke in the fridge.

"I thought you said you made good money," I said. "You can't afford food?"

"Quite the opposite, but I don't like going to the store. I don't like shopping for food either. The store is too loud and too bright. Plus, people are there," he said.

"So, you've been living off chips and Coke since Charlie died?" I asked.

"I'm fine," Rook replied. "You don't have to take care of me."

"That's true, but I do have to take care of me. If you come along for the ride, I'm cool with that," I said.

"What do you mean?" Rook looked perplexed.

"It sucks cooking for one person, so when I make a meal, I'll make enough for two. You're welcome to join me, or you can keep living off Coke and potato chips. I need you around, though, so it would probably be good if you at least occasionally ate some real food," I said. "A vegetable every once in a while would be even better, and fried potatoes of any variety do not count."

"I loathe the grocery store," Rook reminded me. What he did not say was that he could not cook or that he hated it.

"That's fine. I don't. It's not my favorite thing to do, but I'll manage. Tell me where the grocery store is, and I'll go pick up a few things," I said.

"Hang on," Rook said and disappeared from the kitchen.

For the couple of minutes that he was gone, I played with the stove burners and surveyed what cooking tools were available. There were plenty of pots, pans, and utensils to make the basic meals I knew how to prepare.

41

Additionally, there were some fancy gadgets that were way above my skill set, but the internet could help me figure it all out.

It was definitely a selling point for staying. A big, well-stocked kitchen with enough time and money to buy good ingredients was a dream come true for someone who had to budget her money for a monthly chicken nugget and movie night.

Rook came bustling back into the kitchen. "Here," he said and shoved a huge wad of money into my hand.

"What's this?" I asked.

"It's your take from the funeral tonight. In the future, you should probably deposit it into the business account and then pay yourself a salary, but you need money to live off of now, right?" Rook asked. "Or not?"

"I do," I said. "This is all two thousand?"

"It is," he said. "Like I said earlier, I already did the admin work for this funeral. We can go over it later if you want to go to the store now."

"I haven't done the funeral yet," I said. "You're paying me in advance?"

"You're paying you in advance. Technically, it is your money either way," he said. "Plus, I doubt you're going to abscond with the money and disappear. You don't seem like the type."

I still hadn't wrapped my head around the fact that the funeral home was my business, and the money it made was mine too. It was still all happening so fast.

"I guess I'll go to the store then," I said.

"Probably don't take it all," Rook countered.

"Why? It's a small town, right? You think I'm going to get robbed?" I asked jokingly.

Rook looked deadly serious. "It's a safe town, but a new person waving around a stack of cash could bring out the worst in someone."

"You gave it to me," I protested. "Anyway, is there somewhere I can stash the rest until I'm settled?"

"There are safes in some of the bedrooms or the petty cash lockbox in the office," Rook offered.

"Could you put it in the lockbox for me? I want to get to the store. I'm starving. We can go over the room situation later?"

"Yes," he said.

I took a couple hundred dollars out of the stack and handed the rest back to him. It was more than enough to get by for a couple of days until I figured out what the heck was going on.

Before Rook put away the money, he gave me directions to the grocery store. When I got out to my car, I googled it too. After finding the address, I plugged it into the GPS.

As I was putting the car in gear, I looked up the driveway and noticed the two hearses sitting under the carport. I hadn't seen them before because I'd been too focused on the front of the house.

For a brief second, I considered taking one of them to the store. The thought made me chuckle. Rook had said I should let the good people of Fullmourn know who I was right off the bat. It was a fun thought, but inevitably, I put the car in gear and backed out of the driveway. There'd be plenty of time for tooling around the town in a hearse when I wasn't so hungry.

The store was super easy to find, and it seemed that's the way everything would be in my new town. Not only was it a small town, but everything was laid out in an orderly grid. Most of the stores were either in the square or around the perimeter of the town.

I saw several large signs for the Fullmourn Cemetery all directing me to take a left. There was a sign every couple of blocks, and I had to wonder if the cemetery actually ran the entire length of town, or if the locals were just enthusiastic about it. Either way, it was a little bizarre.

The farm and home store next to the grocery store distracted me from my ponderings about the town's graveyard. Running across the front of the store was a list of things you could find inside. In addition to feed and tools, there was something else that piqued my interest.

Clothing.

I really needed to go to the grocery store and head back, but I also didn't want to sleep in my skirt, and I wasn't comfortable enough yet to sleep au naturel. What I needed was some pajamas, or a nightgown, and a change of clothes until I could get back to my apartment. I wasn't sure if I had time before the funeral I was supposed to conduct, and I knew I wouldn't feel like going after.

So, I parked my car at the farm and home store and hurried inside. The double doors whooshed open and the smell of dog food and feed hit me like a Mack truck.

For reasons I couldn't quite explain, the place made me feel a bit nostalgic. It was as if someone had brought me into a place like that when I was a young child. I couldn't really remember it, but it was there buried deep. And just close enough to the surface to make me feel a little sentimental.

I proceeded past the penny candy and tool specials to find the women's clothing section. I was in luck. Not only did I find a soft cotton nightgown that would serve its purpose well, I also found a bag of underwear, a pack of socks, some jeans, and a couple of black t-shirts.

At the register, I was pleased to find that my entire purchase, including a canister of locally made beef jerky, was less than forty dollars. Plus, I got to meet Tammy, the cashier.

"You're not from around here," she said as she looked me over.

"I'm not, but I'm going to be staying for a little while. I'll be running the Holloway and Sons Funeral Home and Crematorium," I said and held my breath for… I don't know. I assumed she'd think I was some sort of freak. I was wrong.

"Oh, yeah?" she said as she bagged my purchases. "You related to Charlie?"

"I'm his great-niece," I said.

"He was real good to my family when my Pawpaw passed," she said. "Any relation to him is all right with me."

"Thank you," I said. "My name's Hazel. It was lovely to meet you, Tammy."

"You too," she said. "Come back again soon."

I probably could have just walked over to the grocery store, but I didn't want to take my bag of clothes inside, so I got my car and changed parking lots. Back in the city, I would have probably put my new purchases in the trunk, but in Fullmourn, it seemed fine to just leave them sitting there on the passenger seat.

My stomach growled as I got out of the car, so I walked inside quickly. I figured I could get in, grab some chicken nuggets and frozen veggies, and get out fast. There would be time later for a more intensive shopping trip.

The inside of the grocery store threw me off. I felt like I'd stepped into a seventies sitcom. The cheesy Muzak played over a staticky PA system. The beige tile flooring beneath my feet looked like typical décor for decades past, but it wasn't the least bit worn or dirty. The best part was the huge orange circles and squares that decorated the walls and hung from the ceilings. Either the store's owner had spent a fortune recreating a retro design for the store, or they had lovingly and meticulously cared for their business for a long time.

I grabbed a basket from the rack inside the doors and followed the signs to the frozen food section. They only had three brands of frozen chicken nuggets, but at least they had my favorite kind. I grabbed a bag and moved down to the vegetables. There I picked up small bags of broccoli and corn. A little further down, I found the frozen fruit, so I tossed a package of blackberries in too. A loaf of bread from a display table in the bakery snuck its way into my basket and brought a small bottle of fancy mayonnaise with it. *Artisan*, the label read. I'd just grabbed it because it was on an endcap. I was sucker for grocery store tricks when I didn't have to stick to my budget.

On my way to the registers, I passed the eggs. They seemed like a good purchase. We'd need something for breakfast, and eggs seemed like a better choice than running out for fast food.

Did Fullmourn even have a fast food place?

I remembered the town did have a coffee shop, café, and bakery.

Coffee.

Good call. I told myself. I couldn't leave the store without coffee.

In the coffee aisle, I picked up a box of sugar packets, a container of creamer, and perused the coffee choices. As I reached out to grab the coffee I'd decided on, someone hit me with their cart.

Mind you, the aisle wasn't packed. I was the only one in it. There was plenty of clearance on either side and all around me, and I confirmed that when the cart struck my butt.

In fact, I looked around again just to make sure I wasn't crazy, and when I turned back to confront the person who had carelessly rammed me with their cart, I found myself face to face with the dude from the gas station. Mr.

Scratch himself. George, I believed his name was...

"Did you just hit me with your cart on purpose?" I asked.

His response was to yank his cart back, and then throw himself on the floor. "Help me!" he cried out, and in my shock, I actually almost tried to help him.

"What are you doing?" I was still completely stunned, and the purpose of his shenanigans hadn't hit me yet.

"Help me!" he cried out again. "She's shoved me down!"

"Are you insane?" I asked and took a step back.

"I think there's a wet spot on this floor too!" he hollered. "Oh, my back!"

Suddenly, there were people in the aisle. There might not have been a ton of them in the store, but they were all there with eyes on me. Fingers flew furiously as they texted, and someone filmed aftermath of the incident with their phone. The whole town might as well have been there. They'd all know about it soon enough. That's how it worked in small towns in movies, and I had no reason to believe that Fullmourn would be any different.

I backed away from the scene even as a store manager showed up and George began squawking about calling the sheriff. I'd briefly considered ditching my basket and running out of the store, but Rook and I still needed groceries. It also would have been rude to just leave the food there to spoil.

Instead, I quickly made my way toward the front of the store to check out. If everyone was over in the coffee aisle fussing over George, then I might have been able to make a quick exit after I paid for my basket's contents.

Of course, right in front of the checkout lanes was a hot food display with rotisserie chickens. They were on sale for five bucks, and seriously, how could I pass that up?

Well, if I had passed it up, then I wouldn't have dropped the first chicken. Which I totally did, and splattered chicken drippings and little bits of meat all over my shoes.

"No..." I let out a half-strangled cry and looked over at the cashier who'd been watching me.

"Clean-up in checkout lane seven," she immediately announced over the PA.

"I'm so sorry," I said. "I really am."

When I turned to step around the destroyed chicken, I ran smack dab into another cashier who'd walked around her station to see what the heck I was doing.

"I'm sorry," I said to her too.

"Ma'am, I can take you here," the cashier in lane seven said. The unspoken part was probably *so you get out of here and stop wrecking things*.

"Thank you," I said and for some reason, grabbed another rotisserie chicken. At least I didn't drop that one. "I'll pay for them both. I'll pay for the one I dropped too."

"That's kind of you, but it's unnecessary. It happens all of the time. The guy that works back in the deli gets grease on the containers, so it's not your fault," she said. Her nametag said Rochelle.

"Really?"

"Really," Rochelle confirmed.

"Thank you," I said.

She was an extraordinarily efficient checkout clerk, and I was out of there in about two minutes. I rushed out of the grocery store and to my car. As I backed out of my space, a cruiser from the Coyote County Sheriff's Department pulled into the lot.

For a brief moment, I contemplated staying and explaining myself, but ultimately decided against it. Why should I? I hadn't done anything wrong, and I was sure that any security footage in the store would prove it.

The man behind the wheel of the cruiser eyed me as we crossed paths. His dark gaze unnerved me, and I was relieved as soon as I was out of his sight.

I was distracted but managed to make it back to the funeral home without crashing my car. The kitchen was a different situation. Rook wasn't around when I started my attempt to prepare us a quick, easy meal of chicken nuggets and baby broccoli florets, but he appeared quickly after I dropped the cookie sheet the third time.

"Are you okay?" he asked as he pried the pan from my hand.

I proceeded to tell him the entire story of my shopping trip and my run-in with George. "But other than that, I'm just peachy," I said when I'd told him everything.

"Do you think you can pour us some Coke without spilling it?" he asked.

"Ha-ha," I retorted. "I need to make us dinner."

By that point, he was meticulously laying out the chicken nuggets in neat little rows. "I've got this if you can get the drinks. There's a bottle of good whiskey behind the salad bowls in the bottom cabinet next to the refrigerator if you want a nip to calm your nerves," he said.

"I have to do a funeral later," I said.

"No law against having a little liquid courage in your veins when you do it," he said. "I'd like a splash in mine too, if you don't mind."

"I didn't see that coming," I said as I searched for, and found, the bottle of whiskey.

"You better learn fast that in this business, everyone will surprise you," he said with what almost sounded like a real chuckle.

"It was my second run-in with that George guy today," I said and took a full on swig right from the bottle of whiskey. It was good stuff. "He was scratching off his scratcher tickets at the counter when I stopped at a gas station earlier. He got all salty with me when I asked him to step aside so I could pay."

"That sounds like George Cadell. Just so you know, lots of people in this town hate him. He's a jerk for sure," Rook said.

"I suppose that should make me feel better, but I think I've made an enemy," I said. "I think he's going to cause problems for me if I can't avoid him."

"I'm sure he'll move on," Rook said. "Probably sooner than you think."

Chapter Six

After we ate, it was time to start getting ready for the funeral. "I've got to bring the body up and get it ready for viewing," Rook said. He was washing the few dishes we'd used, and I was drying them.

"Oh," I said.

"Don't tell me you're getting squeamish now," he said and looked at me with a pointed expression. There was a little divot in the space between his eyebrows.

"No. Nothing like that. I'm used to bodies, but I'm anxious about the actual funeral tonight. I think it's more the idea of having to deal with live people that's got me nervous. They'll be grieving. There will be emotions. In my former job, it was just the bodies," I said.

"Like I told you before, I don't think anyone is coming tonight. I'll stick around, though. I'm not very good with people, but I can hang out for moral support," Rook said.

"Are you sure?" I asked.

"It's not like I have anything better to do," he said. "If I didn't stay here with you, then I'd be going up to my room to play video games or chess."

"Thank you," I said.

"Okay, then," Rook declared as I dried the last plate and put it away in the cabinet, "it's time to see the elevator."

"There's an elevator?" I asked.

"Did you think I was going to carry the body upstairs in a sack?" he asked.

The visual of said act made me giggle despite myself. "No."

"So, the casket is already downstairs. I generally like to take the casket downstairs and put the body in it where no one can see, and then I bring the whole thing up. I suppose that I could bring the deceased up and arrange them up here, but then we run the risk of someone walking in off the street and seeing that," Rook said as he left the kitchen and we walked down a short hallway.

At the end of that hallway was a metal door. Rook pushed a button next to the doorframe, and the elevator opened. It wasn't as big as you'd find in a hospital or commercial building. There was room for us both to ride down, but I had my doubts that there was space for the two of us and the casket to make the trip back upstairs.

The doors closed, and the elevator didn't move. Rook pulled a key out of his pocket and inserted it into a lock above a button that said "B".

"There's a key to get down to the morgue and staging area," Rook said. "You'll find one in your desk. It's necessary because we don't want anyone getting in the elevator and going downstairs."

"Has that happened?" I asked as we began our descent.

"That's why Charlie had the elevator upgraded a few years ago," Rook said, but he didn't elaborate further.

I was going to press him because it had to be an interesting story, but we were already in the basement. The doors opened, Rook removed the key, and slipped it back into his pocket.

The basement wasn't as dark as I'd expected. There also wasn't any buffer between us and the morgue. The elevator doors opened up, and we were in a huge, white tiled room.

"Does the morgue take up the entire basement?" I asked as we stepped out of the elevator.

"For the most part," he said. "There's a bathroom and a small breakroom down here too. I don't like to have to come upstairs when I'm working, so everything I need for an entire day's work is down here."

"You don't come upstairs to eat?" I asked.

"The breakroom has a fridge and microwave. As you can imagine, I've got it stocked with Coke and chips right now," Rook said as we proceeded over to a casket on a cart. It was closed, and I got this weird sense of impending doom when I looked at it. I knew there was a body inside. What I didn't understand was why that made me feel uneasy.

Maybe not seeing her was worse than just having her laid out on the table.

"So, we're just taking the casket upstairs and putting it in the viewing room?" I confirmed.

"Yes, but as you probably noticed, there's only room in the elevator for one person and the casket. So, I'll stay behind while you take her upstairs," Rook offered.

"Are you sure?" I asked.

"Of course," he said. "As long as you're up for pushing her out of the elevator, and then don't forget to come back down and get me."

"I should have gotten my key before we did this," I said.

"It's fine. Just remember to keep it on you later," Rook said with a shrug. "All right, get in."

"What?" For a moment, a vision of him killing me and stuffing me in a casket flashed through my mind. The place was giving me a worse case of the heebie-jeebies than I expected.

"To the elevator," he said. "Get in the elevator, and I'll push the casket into you. It will be easier than you riding up with your back pressed against the doors and then trying to drag the casket out. They are easier to push."

"Oh, right," I said and went back to the elevator.

I waited inside while Rook rolled the cart over to me. He pushed it into the elevator, put his key in the lock, and then pressed the button for the first floor.

"Going up," Rook said as the doors closed.

I hated elevators, a fact that I'd been too distracted to remember until I was stuffed into one with a giant casket. It suddenly felt like the walls were closing in on me, and for a split second, I could have sworn I heard the old woman moving around inside the casket.

Fortunately, the doors opened before I could really work myself into a tizzy, and I shoved the cart as hard as I could. We were out of the elevator and into the hallway in moments.

Was I supposed to leave her in the hallways and go back down for Rook? Or was I supposed to wheel her to the viewing room and then go get him? That was something we should have worked out beforehand.

Ultimately, I decided to leave her in the hallway and go back down for him right away. I was still completely new to the house, and thought I was fairly sure I knew the way to the viewing room, I didn't want to chance getting lost.

While pushing a casket.

"I'll be right back," I said to the casket. "Why am I talking to you?" I asked and turned for the elevator. "And I'm asking you why I'm talking to you. I've lost it."

You really have...

The disembodied voice sent a chill down my spine. Again, I thought I heard something move inside the casket.

The doors closed, and I'd never ever been so happy to be in an elevator. When they opened in the basement, the morgue was empty.

I rubbed my eyes as if I were having some sort of bad dream. Was I sleeping? Had I actually gotten into a car accident and was in a coma?

A sense of relief washed over me when I heard a familiar sound. It was the noise a bag of chips makes when someone rips it open, and it was coming from one of the two doors off the morgue.

"We just ate dinner," I called out.

Rook appeared in the doorway. "I like chips," he said with a shrug.

"Obviously," I answered. "I left her in the hallway upstairs. I guess we better get back up there and get things arranged. Are you bringing the chips?"

"No one's up there, right?" he asked.

"Nope. Not that I saw… or heard," I was not telling him that I was hearing voices.

"Then it's fine," he said. "I'll drop these off in the kitchen on the way."

I didn't think I'd ever seen someone shovel potato chips in their face the way Rook did on the ride back upstairs. I couldn't believe that someone who could put away fried foods like that would be a skinny as he was. Men. Wasn't the least bit fair, in my opinion.

He did drop the chips off in the kitchen, washed his hands, and then I followed as he wheeled the casket into the viewing room. Once he had it in place, I watched as Rook lifted the lid.

"She's all ready," he said. "Most funerals have more flowers than this, but I wanted to stay in the budget. Do you think they are okay?"

I looked around at the three bouquets he'd placed at either side of the casket. Two on one side and one on the other. "Moonflowers?" I asked.

"They seemed fitting for some reason," he said. "Plus they were on sale."

"She looks peaceful," I said. "You do a good job."

"Thank you," Rook returned.

"Well, now what?" I asked.

"We have an hour or so. Why don't I show you to your office? You can get your elevator key, and then we'll come back here and wait," he said.

"Sounds good to me."

My office was more than I expected. It looked like it belonged to someone important. I could hardly believe that I would ever belong in there.

The desk was massive, and it was in the center of the humongous room. The walls were lined with floor-to-ceiling bookshelves. They mostly contained books, but there was the odd decoration. And by decoration, I mean skulls.

"Are those real?" I asked.

"I don't know," Rook answered. "I never asked. Charlie had his quirks."

"I see," I said as I examined another one of the decorations on the shelf to the right of my desk. It was an old globe. Outdated, but too beautiful to even think about throwing away.

"I can remove them if they bother you," Rook offered.

"No, it's fine. They're a little weird, but I don't mind. This is a lot of books," I said.

"Most of them are related to the industry in one way or another. There are textbooks, various other non-fiction books on the funeral industry, some anatomy and physiology stuff, and of course, novels."

"Novels about funerals?" I asked.

"Some. Others are just about death in general. You'll find the complete collection of Edgar Alan Poe works over there," he said and pointed to a shelf by the window.

"This is a lot," I said.

Rook moved around behind the desk and opened one of the drawers. "Here's your elevator key," he said and handed me a key on a length of black ribbon. "And here's the one for petty cash." Another key tied to a piece of green string.

"Color coded," I observed before shoving them into my skirt pocket.

"I never thought about it," he said. "You can stay in here and look around a bit, or we can go... wait."

"Let's just go. I want to be there in case someone shows up early, and I don't really like the idea of just leaving the deceased unattended like that," I said.

"Why?" Rook questioned, but we'd already began walking for the door.

"What if someone walks in and... I don't know... like, messes with her or something. There are a lot of very strange people out there, and I'm sure word got out that the funeral home was changing hands."

"I locked the door after you came in," Rook said. "We have to unlock the front doors for the viewing."

"Oh," I said.

"Yep. Best to keep them locked unless you know someone is coming. There are a lot of strange people out there."

"What if someone comes here to inquire?" I asked.

"Well, usually they call first. Or, we get a call from the hospital or county morgue first. If someone does drop in, and that rarely happens, they can ring the bell," Rook said.

"Makes sense."

Rook had been right. No one showed up for the woman's funeral. We sat there the entire time, and not one car even drove down the street.

It was the longest two hours I could remember. We couldn't get on our phones or play a game of cards just in case someone walked in, so we literally just had to stand there. Well, Rook sat in the back. He'd taken a seat in the last row of chairs and to his credit, he sat there almost the entire time.

There was once when he said he needed to run to the restroom, but I was pretty sure he'd gone into the kitchen to eat chips. I stood at the door and waited.

When it was over, Rook closed the casket and started to wheel her away. He was taking her back to the elevator and then downstairs.

"Will there be a burial?" I asked. "You didn't mention one."

"She's being cremated. The casket is just a loaner," he said.

"You're going to do that now?" I asked.

"The crematory is out back. It's a gray brick building out the back doors. It looks like a big garage with a smoke stack," he said.

"Should I come with you?" I asked.

"I can do this part. You stay here in case we get any stragglers. It's not that late. Throw the flowers out, dust the chairs, and then vacuum," he said. "You can hire a housekeeper to come in and do that stuff, but Charlie always did it himself."

"I don't mind," I said. "How long should I wait?"

"Give it another half an hour, and then do the cleaning. Make sure you lock the doors and turn off the porch lights. That will discourage anyone from even ringing the bell after the sun is completely set," he said.

"You sure you don't want me to come with you?" I asked.

"I'm not scared, but you seem a bit skittish. I'm kind of surprised," Rook said.

"I am too," I admitted. I'd been in far spookier situations, and the deceased wasn't my first body by a long shot.

"Better get used to it," he said. "I'll show you the cremation process the next time. You've had a big day. When I'm finished, I'll show you the available rooms and the apartment."

"Sounds good," I said, and then I was alone.

I waited the half hour, and no one came. So, I gathered the flowers and headed for the kitchen. Rook hadn't told me where to throw them away, but I figured if the crematory was out back, perhaps there was a dumpster too.

The door off the kitchen was more of a side door than a back door. I went out and made my way around the house with the armful of moonflowers. Sure enough, I found a green dumpster.

I opened the black lid and chucked the flowers in. When it closed, I looked off in the distance.

The crematory was a wide, squat building. There were two small windows on the side I could see, and smoke was starting to come out of the chimney.

"Goodbye," I said. "I'm sorry no one showed up for you."

I made my way back inside the house and retrieved a rag from the kitchen. I figured I'd wipe down the chairs in the viewing room, and then start my search for the vacuum. Rook hadn't actually told me where to find it, so I was going to have to start opening doors. There were potential closets everywhere, and I wasn't sure what doors were storage and what were actual rooms. I had a lot to learn.

But, I had a rag, and figured I'd worry about one thing at a time. It only took me a few minutes to dust all the chairs, so I went around and wiped down any wood trim and the baseboards. They probably didn't need to be done all the time, but I figured it was better to give them a frequent swipe than to have to get down on my knees and scrub them. Neglect just made more work later.

After tossing the rag back in the kitchen because I had no idea where the washer and dryer were, I began my search for a vacuum cleaner.

I managed to find three closets that didn't have a vacuum and another huge room that appeared to be a second viewing room without locating a sweeper. As I turned a corner and found myself wandering down another hallway, the hairs on the back of my neck stood up.

There was someone behind me, and I knew it before I even turned around. Had I locked the front doors before I started my dusting? It would have been just my luck that on my first day, some psycho wandered in off the street and was stalking me through the funeral home.

Or, it could have just been Rook and I was letting my imagination get the better of me. To be fair, though, that place was spooky as heck. I'd worked with the dead my entire adult life, and Holloway and Sons Funeral Home was still a bit eerie.

I turned around to see who was behind me, and my heart dropped into my stomach. "I'm in a zombie movie," I blurted out without thinking.

Then she laughed at me. It was then I realized she was kinda see-through. It was for sure the woman whose funeral I'd just unsuccessfully conducted, but she was a tad transparent.

"What is going on?" I asked and then prayed she didn't actually answer.

I rubbed my eyes and hoped when I opened them again, she'd be gone. She wasn't, though, she was still standing there smiling at me.

Even with my heart thundering in my chest, I began to pick up little details about her presence that I hadn't noticed at first. Her face was smoother and the black dress she wore wasn't the one she'd been wearing in the casket. And… this part is crazy… but her hair seemed to be turning from silver to a lustrous shade of black.

I was losing my mind.

Or, I really was in a coma having some sort of weird dream.

"Annabelle?" I asked when she still refused to disappear.

"The one and only," she said. "Well, probably not, but that's neither here nor there right now."

"Am I dead?" I asked. "Is this like purgatory or something?"

She laughed again. "No, dear. You're not dead. I most certainly am, though."

"Then, why are you standing there?" I couldn't believe I was having a conversation with her instead of running in terror, but I found her presence oddly compelling. My feet were rooted in place, and at the same time, I felt drawn to the woman before me.

"Well, I don't want to be. That's for dang sure," she said. "But, no one from my good-for-nothing family bothered to show up for my funeral."

"I'm sorry about that," I said.

"I am too, but it's your lucky day," she said and rubbed her hands together.

"What?"

As she rubbed her hands together, Annabelle's spirit took on an unearthly glow. That's a stupid way to describe it because obviously she was a ghost, but I don't know what else to say about the matter. She smile, rubbed her hands together, and her spirit began to radiate with a brilliant shade of white light.

"Well, dear, I'm a witch. That wouldn't matter to you except that I have to pass my magic onto someone else before I can cross over to the other side. I'm supposed to gift my powers to a member of my family, but none of them bothered to show up. So, it's your lucky day, Hazel. I'm tired and I want to move on. You're here, so if I give them to you, I don't have to roam the Earth looking for someone. It's win-

win for us both," she said and moved closer to me.

"What are you doing?" I asked and held my hands up in front of me like it was going to protect me.

"I just told you. I'm giving you my magic," she said. "Use it well."

I took a step back and tried to will my feet to run, but it did no good. The light emanating from Annabelle's body turned to tentacles and snaked across the distance between us.

While I braced myself for pain, I don't know why but I did, the light wrapped itself around my fingers and wrists. From there it moved up my arms until it reached my shoulders. I couldn't really see what it was doing after that because one of those light appendages covered my eyes.

All I could see was that brilliant white light. For the umpteenth time that day, I convinced myself I was dead.

But I was also calm. My heart had slowed, and the light didn't hurt. It didn't sting. In fact, it was warm and fuzzy as it encompassed my entire body. Though I could no longer see it, I could feel its warm embrace.

That's what it ultimately felt like. It was a warm hug from your favorite person, and when my eyes cleared, I could still feel that light inside of me. It was almost as if I could reach down into myself and grab that light if I needed it.

But that was crazy talk.

"What are you doing?" Rook was standing at the end of the hallway looking at me like I was nuts.

"I don't... I think..." I hesitated because I could not tell him what had just happened. He'd think I was a nutcase. Rook would walk me out to my car and wish me well on my way if he knew that I was seeing, and talking, to dead people. "I think I might have just had some sort of seizure," I said.

"Do you have a history of seizures?" Rook asked.

"No," I said.

"Probably just stress," he said. "You've had a big day."

"You're right," I said. "I think I'm dehydrated too. I've had Coke and whiskey, but I can't recall drinking any water today."

"Well, then let's get you some water, and I'll show you the rooms. You should probably rest."

"I still need to vacuum," I said. "I was looking for the vacuum."

"Well, you were almost there," he said. "Up there on the left is where we keep it, but you can move it to a different closet if you want. You can also wait and vacuum tomorrow. We don't have any more services scheduled, so it won't hurt to leave it until tomorrow. Just not too early."

"All right," I said. "Well, let's look at the rooms."

There were five bedrooms on the second floor. Three were on the front side of the house and two larger rooms on the back. One of those two was a bit larger than the other and also had a huge en suite bathroom.

Upstairs on the third floor was an apartment and a storage area. I walked through the apartment thinking that it was the natural choice, but I just didn't feel like staying there.

"I think I like the big bedroom on the second floor," I said. "The one with the black tile bathroom."

"You don't want the apartment? You'd have your own kitchen and laundry," Rook said.

"There's no other washer and dryer in the house?" I asked.

"No, there is. There's a laundry room on the first floor. I use it, but we could share," he said. "Or you can use the washer and dryer in the apartment even if you don't stay there."

"I really like that bedroom," I said.

It had been decorated like something out of a castle. A goth castle with just a hint of vampire aesthetic. The gigantic four-poster bed sat in the middle of the room, and there was a huge window overlooking the back yard.

Black drapes hung from ornate rods, and beneath them were a set of black-out curtains that could be closed to keep out intrusive sunshine. The carpet was thick and a deep shade of burgundy. I wanted to kick my shoes off and walk around in it because it was so plush that you sunk down a little bit when you stepped on it.

There were more bookshelves too. Five in all, and they were lined with books of every genre. "Charlie liked to collect books," Rook said when I walked over to peruse the titles.

"Was this his room?"

"No," Rook said. "No one has really used this room since Charlie's grandmother. Or perhaps it was his great-grandmother. Either way, he just put books on the shelves in here. Those cases are heavy, so he had no desire to move them."

"It's very clean. Charlie cleaned this whole house without help?"

"He did. We have long stretches where there's no work to do. He said it kept him fit, so he did it himself," Rook answered.

"Long stretches with no work? You said that there's at least a funeral a week," I said.

"Charlie didn't have many hobbies other than reading. He didn't like computers or watch television. He also only slept a few hours a night, so one funeral a week was not enough to keep him busy," Rook said.

"I see," I responded. "Well, I think I'm going to take this room if that's okay with you."

"Not up to me, Hazel. This house is yours. You can take all the rooms if you like. You can sleep in a different one every night, but I'd prefer if I could keep the tower," Rook said.

"You mentioned that before, and of course I'm not going to kick you out of your room. Any chance you might let me see it someday? I don't think I've ever been in a house with a tower," I said.

"We'll see," he said with a tight smile that I immediately interpreted as a no. "Do you need anything else? I'd like to turn in for the night. I do like computers, and I've got a project I'm in the middle of right now."

"No, please go. I'll be fine. I think I even remember the way to the kitchen," I said.

"And you know where the bathroom is," Rook added as he headed out the door. "Open or closed?"

"Closed, please," I said, and he shut the door quietly behind him.

The house was quiet. It was instantly unnerving. I was used to living in a small city where I could hear people outside coming and going and hear my neighbors.

Holloway and Sons was solidly built, and I couldn't even hear Rook walking down the hall. Probably had something to do with the bedroom's oak door. I didn't think I'd ever lived in a place that didn't have those hollow-core doors. The ones where you could hear everything.

I took the bags with my purchases over to the bedroom's dresser and plopped them down on top. My face stared back at me from the giant mirror affixed to the wall behind the chest of drawers. I pulled the elastics out of my black hair and ran my fingers through until I looked like a wild animal.

I had a brush in my purse but laid out on a silver platter at one end of the dresser was a boar's hairbrush, comb, and hand mirror. "I guess these are mine too," I said as I picked up the heavy brush and ran the bristles through my hair.

In my new bathroom, I brushed my teeth and washed my face before slipping into the pajamas I'd purchased earlier in the day. There was nothing left to do but go to bed.

Or I could go exploring.

I hadn't gotten that good of a look at the house yet, and my curiosity was at war with anxiety. The house kind of creeped me out, but that made it even more intriguing.

"You saw a ghost," I said as I stood at my bedroom door. My hand was poised in the air waiting for me to decide if I was going to reach out and turn the knob or go to bed. "You didn't really see a ghost," I said to the door. "I mean, that couldn't have really happened. Don't be crazy."

"Yeah, don't be crazy," a voice said from behind me.

I whirled around and no one was there. "I am really losing it," I said. I had never heard of anyone having a psychotic break come out of absolutely nowhere, but I figured it had to happen. Right? Maybe Rook had poisoned me. Perhaps he'd dosed my chicken nuggets with LSD. I had no idea why someone would do something like that, but he was quirky.

"Honey, you already lost it," the voice said.

My eyes frantically searched the room for the source of the words. The voice was different from when I'd hallucinated Annabelle's ghost. So, I knew I must be having a new hallucination, but what was it?

"Can't be," I said when I located the source of the snark.

"Oh, but it can," it said.

"You're a mouse," I said.

"You're brilliant," he retorted.

I only say he because the voice, the mousy voice, sounded more masculine. Not that I'd seen any mice ever talk before, but I was basing it on cartoons.

"I should go to the emergency room. I am having a psychotic break," I said to myself and not the mouse who was not and could not be talking to me.

Mice did not talk.

Ghosts did not walk the halls of the funeral home handing out magical powers.

"You should probably just go to bed," the mouse said. "You've had a long day."

The idea to catch the mouse came into my head. If I could grab him, I could take him upstairs to Rook's room. If Rook could hear him talk, then I wasn't crazy.

So, I did the only rational thing. I lunged at the mouse and tried to grab him.

"Whoa, lady," he said as he turned and scurried for a hole in the baseboard.

I dove for him and missed as he scurried into the wall from which he came. What I also did was overshoot and crack my head against the wall.

So, there I was lying on the floor, probably with a head injury, and my eyes were lined up perfectly with the little hole the mouse had come through. I could see him inside staring back at me with his little black eyes.

He looked... concerned.

There was something else too. It had to have been the LSD I'd been poisoned with or the head injury, or my new case of psychosis, but I could have sworn the little guy had wings.

Not like mouse wings either. They were like... fairy wings. Ethereal almost. Tiny but otherworldly and beautiful. The little bit of light filtering through the hole made them sparkle with shades of pink, purple, and brilliant gold.

I had lost my ever-loving mind.

Chapter Seven

I woke up the next morning in my pajamas lying on the floor of a strange, but magnificent, bedroom. For a moment, I thought all of my fantasies had finally come true, and I'd been kidnapped by a rich and gorgeous vampire.

That did not sparkle.

Or that did. I wasn't going to be that picky.

As I picked myself up off the floor, it started to come back to me where I was and what I was doing there. I was in the new funeral home that I owned, but why was I on the floor?

Rook and I had some whiskey before the funeral, I'd need to take it easy with the sauce. I wasn't a big drinker, and apparently that little bit of booze had done me in big time.

The dreams were the strangest part. I wasn't accustomed to weird dreams. But the night before, I'd dreamt of the deceased coming back and turning me into a witch. As I headed to the bathroom, I recalled a second dream about a talking fairy mouse.

"No more whiskey," I said to my bathroom reflection. "You obviously cannot hold your liquor."

After brushing my teeth and getting dressed in the jeans and t-shirt I'd purchased at the farm and home store, I headed downstairs to see about breakfast. Despite having been so drunk that I passed out on the floor and had super weird dreams, I wasn't the least bit queasy. In fact, I was starving.

I pulled on a pair of socks before leaving the bedroom and headed out to find the kitchen and make some eggs and toast. The house was completely silent as I made my way downstairs.

Rook had said he had some big computer project he wanted to work on, so my guess was that he'd stayed up late. I assumed he wouldn't be joining me for breakfast.

They say that you remember things better after you sleep on them, and that was true of the house's layout. I easily found my way back to the kitchen. It couldn't have had anything to do with the fact that it was probably going to be my favorite room in the house…

As soon as I was in the kitchen, I put a pot of coffee on. After grabbing a skillet and some butter, I cracked a couple of eggs into the pan and put some bread in the toaster. By the time it was all done, the kitchen smelled incredible. There's nothing quite like the scent of buttery eggs, fresh toast, and strong coffee mingled together on a relaxing morning.

Of course, I chowed through the food in record time, and when I was done washing my dishes, I realized I needed something to do. There was vacuuming.

Would it bother Rook?

I doubted it because he was all the way up on the fourth floor. I figured I'd give it a shot, and if the vacuum was too loud, I'd just wait.

A strange feeling came over me as I walked down the hall to retrieve the sweeper. My dream from the night before came crashing back into my mind. It was the same hallway where the dead woman appeared behind me.

I knew that it was just a nightmare my brain had made up, but I couldn't help checking over my shoulder constantly. I grabbed the vacuum from the closet and hurried back to the viewing room.

Of course, no ghost ever appeared. I quickly vacuumed the carpet in the viewing room and the hall. It wasn't that loud, so I just did it as fast as I could.

Rook never appeared looking grumpy, so he must not have heard it. I looked at the clock. It was still pretty early, and I couldn't do any more work until Rook showed me the ropes.

One thing I did need to do was go back to my apartment and pack some things. I'd need to arrange a moving van as well. Getting my car and a moving van back to Fullmourn would require two people, but at the very least, I could bring what fit in my car and make the reservation.

I left a note for Rook on the kitchen table that said I'd gone back to my apartment to fetch some things and I'd be back as soon as possible. I also needed to get some more groceries. Maybe some steaks. I could cook a delicious meal and use it to bribe Rook into helping me move.

On my way out the front door and to my car, I nearly tripped over some garbage bags someone had dumped on the porch in the middle of the night. Except that it wasn't garbage bags.

It was a body.

Now, I'd worked with bodies for a long time, and normally they didn't freak me out, but finding a random one on your porch is a different story. Especially when you kicked it. At least I'd put on shoes because I was leaving, but still.

For a second, I thought perhaps I was overreacting. Could people just leave a body for us that way? Did Holloway and Sons offer some sort of drop-off service? Was our front porch like the book drop at the library?

That was stupid. Even I could admit it, but again, finding a body that way was shocking.

I gingerly stepped over him and got out my phone. The most hilarious part of the entire ordeal was that I was still trying to be quiet so I didn't wake up Rook.

Even when I called 911, I whispered until the dispatcher told me I needed to speak up unless I was in danger.

"I don't think I'm in danger," I said and quickly scanned the front yard and the driveway. "Unless the killer is still here? Do you think the killer could still be here?"

"Ma'am, you're going to have to back up a little," the dispatcher said.

"Okay, so I'm on my front porch. I was getting ready to leave to go to my old apartment, and there is a body right outside my front door," I said. "I think I need the police."

"Are you sure the person is dead?" The dispatcher asked.

"I... I mean, they look pretty dead. Hold on," I said and knelt down to feel for a pulse. He was as cold as ice, and there was sadly no pulse. "Yeah, he's dead for sure."

"And you say he was murdered?" The dispatcher asked.

"I mean... I assume so. Otherwise, why would he be here on my porch being dead? We don't offer drive-through services here," I said because of course we didn't.

"Excuse me?" she asked.

"I'm at Holloway and Sons Funeral Home. There is a dead body on the front porch, and I didn't leave it here. I suppose he could have had a heart attack or something. I don't know for sure, but I assume murder. Can you please send police?"

"Ma'am, the sheriff is already en route to your location. I would like to keep you on the phone until he arrives in case there is someone there who wishes to harm you," the dispatcher said.

"Should I go back in the house?" I asked.

"Yes, and lock the door. Don't come out until the sheriff is there," she said.

I did as she asked. After gingerly stepping back over George Cadell's body, I went inside and locked the front door.

"Okay, I'm back inside. Do you know how long it will be before the sheriff arrives?" I asked.

"He's in the area, so it shouldn't be more than a few minutes," the dispatcher said.

"My cousin is here. He's sleeping upstairs. I suppose I should go get him," I said.

"Yes, you probably should, but stay on the line with me," she said.

"Okay, got it. I don't work out much, so I don't know if I can talk and climb three flights of stairs. Please just hang in with me. You'll know I'm still on the line by the heavy breathing," I said.

She did not laugh.

Surprisingly, I did not get nearly as winded running up the stairs as I thought I would. In my mind, it was because my adrenaline was spiking. Finding a deceased person could do that to you.

At the top of the stairs, there was one door across a small landing. I knocked on it. "I'm knocking on his door now," I said to the dispatcher.

"Hurry up and get back downstairs," she said. "You'll want to be ready when the sheriff arrives."

Duh. But I didn't say that. She was doing her job.

Rook didn't answer, so I knocked again. Then again. The fourth time I practically pounded on the door.

Finally, the door opened a crack, and a very grumpy-looking Rook peeked out. "What is it?" His voice was gravely and his hair stuck up in every direction.

"There's a dead person on the front porch," I said.

"What? We didn't have any appointments scheduled today," he said.

"Do people drop off bodies on the front porch by appointment?" I asked.

"Wait... no. What? What's going on?" Rook looked like he was finally waking up.

"I'm on the phone with 911 and the sheriff is on the way," I said. "There's a body on the porch. I have to get back downstairs and wait for the police. Get dressed and meet me down there."

He shut the door, and I ran back down the stairs. The front door had a big glass pane in the top half, so I was able to look out and confirm that the body was still there. Also, the sheriff's cruiser was on our street.

I waited until it turned into the driveway and started to open the door. Then, I remembered that forensics was a thing that existed. I'd already messed up the scene before, but that had been an accident. There was no good reason for me to make it worse.

Instead of going out the front, I ran through the house to the kitchen and went out the side door. I was stepping down the small set of concrete stairs onto the driveway as the sheriff, or who I assumed was the sheriff, was getting out of his cruiser.

"He's here," I said to the dispatcher. "I can hang up now?"

"I've confirmed his location, and yes. Good luck," she said and the line disconnected.

I shoved my phone into the pocket of my jeans and walked down the driveway to meet the sheriff. To say that he wasn't what I expected would have been an understatement.

Unconsciously, my hands flew up to fidget with my hair. I smoothed it down the best I could and felt utterly self-conscious without makeup. Meeting a man that good-looking when you're wearing a t-shirt and baggy jeans is kind of a nightmare.

So is finding a dead body, I thought.

My brain was right. It didn't matter that the county sheriff looked like he'd stepped off a movie set. There were more important things at hand.

"Are you the new owner?" he asked and tipped his hat to me.

"I am. I'm Hazel. Hazel Holloway," I said and blushed when my voice cracked. I was squawking like a dying frog because Sheriff McHottie was making me nervous.

"It's nice to meet you, Ms. Holloway. I wish it were under better circumstances," he said and offered me a soft smile. "My name is Sheriff Nicodemus Quillen. Most people around these parts call me Nico."

It was disarming, to say the least. His skin was naturally tan, and it made his perfect teeth look blindly white. The full lips and razor-sharp jawline didn't hurt either.

"It is nice to meet you too," I manage to squeak out. "Thank you for coming."

"It is my job," he said and shut his cruiser door.

"Oh, right," I said and felt myself blush furiously. "So, I woke Rook up, and I assume he'll be downstairs soon."

"The body is on the front porch?" he asked and nodded in that direction.

"It is," I said. "Um.. What should I do?"

"Just wait here for now. Or you can go inside and ask Rook to use the side door," he said.

But even as he said it, Rook came shuffling out the side door. He made his way down the driveway toward me as Nico strode up the front sidewalk to the porch. They offered each other a wave as they crossed latitudes.

"That's George Cadell," Rook said.

"I know. It's weird isn't it?" I said, but I was more focused on watching Nico walk up the stairs. He clearly spent a lot of time doing squats at the gym, and it wasn't my fault that I could not peel my eyes from his exquisite derriere.

"Did you kill him?" Rook asked, and I laughed.

When I turned to look at my cousin, he wasn't amused. "Oh, you're not joking..."

"Well?" Rook asked.

"Seriously, Rook?" I couldn't hide my exasperation. "Charlie chose me because he believed in me, right? I doubt he would have thought so highly of me if I was a killer."

"He didn't really know you, Hazel. He studied you from afar. He thought you were impressive on paper, but we didn't really know you," Rook said.

"I did not kill George. He was annoying and awful, but I'm not the type to kill someone over having to wait a long time at a gas station," I said.

"He did hit you with a shopping cart," Rook offered.

"I still wouldn't kill someone. I would have liked to have slapped him silly, but murder was never on the table," I said.

"Okay, good," Rook looked like he believed me. "Because a lot of people who are comfortable working with the dead are also kind of crazy."

"That's rude," I said.

"Hey, it applies to me too. I'm not saying all people who do what we do, but there are some nutters using it as cover," he said.

"I'm not one of them, I assure you," I said.

But was that the truth? I definitely didn't think I was a killer, but my mental health over the last couple of days could have been called into question.

You're not hallucinating. I told myself. *Those were just dreams.*

Nico made his way back over to us. "I can get a warrant, but it would be a great deal easier if you would just give me permission to search the house," he said.

"Of course," Rook replied instantly.

"I need her permission, right?" Nico said, and I felt my heart flutter. I had become an idiot. Just a puddle of idiocy over a good-looking man.

"I suppose you do," Rook said. "Well?" He looked at me.

"Yes. We've got nothing to hide," I said way more defensively than I intended.

So, it began. Rook and I waited there in the driveway for more deputies to show up and secure the scene. Once they had, Nico and one of his men went inside and began the long process of searching the house. I was glad that I'd eaten breakfast. I just wished I could go to the apartment and get some things done instead of standing in the driveway.

Eventually, Nico and his deputy came back out of the house. The county coroner came and picked up the body. The deputies dispersed, but Nico stayed behind.

"I'll need to take your statement," he said to me. "Rook, I'll need yours as well."

"I was sleeping," he said.

"Okay, well, I can write that up," Nico replied. "I still need to speak to you." He'd turned to address me. His eyes were piercing, but in an intense way that suddenly made me uncomfortable.

"Well, that's my signal," Rook said. "If either of you need me, I'll be inside."

"What's going on?" I asked Nico when Rook was out of earshot.

"I know that you and George had some issues," he said.

"We didn't have issues," I said defensively. "I didn't even know the man."

"You know that I saw you leaving the grocery store after George had his incident. He said you pushed him, and then you were seen fleeing the scene," Nico said, but his voice was flat and gave nothing away. I had no idea if he seriously believed I'd pushed George and was bolting.

"I didn't push him," I said.

"People around here took your actions to mean you were guilty," Nico said.

"The store doesn't have security cameras?" I asked.

"It does," Nico answered.

"Then you know I didn't push him," I said.

"I do," Nico confirmed. "But some might say that was a motive for murder."

"That's insane," I retorted. "You really think that someone would kill a person for something stupid like that?"

"I'm sure people have killed for less," Nico answered.

"Well, I'm not that kind of person. I'm not an insane person. That old man was trying to get attention and probably money. My guess is he wanted to sue the grocery store. You know that I saw him earlier in the day at the gas station outside of town. He was scratching his lottery tickets at the counter blocking the line," I said.

"So, you had two run-ins with the victim in one day?" Nico asked with one eyebrow cocked high.

"No!" He was frustrating me to no end, but it didn't take me long to figure out that's exactly what he was trying to do. What I didn't know was if it was for professional or recreational purposes. A man that hot could not be a nice guy too. That only happened in Hallmark movies. "I mean… I did, but not like what you're saying. I ran into him twice and he was a huge jerk both times, but that's not a reason to kill someone. Not in my book anyway."

"But there are reasons in your book to kill someone?" Nico asked.

I took a deep breath. "No. Never. Look, I don't know what you want me to say. I'm trying here."

"I don't want you to try. I just want the truth," Nico said.

"Well, I'm telling you the truth. I didn't kill George Cadell, and I have no idea how he ended up on the porch of the funeral home. I wish I could help you, but I can't," I said.

He asked me a few more procedural questions. I showed him my driver's license and told him that Rook could confirm my alibi. "Okay. I think that's all I need from you right now, Ms. Holloway. Don't leave town, though," Nico instructed.

"I need to go to my old apartment and get some things," I said. "Is that okay? I'm coming back to Fullmourn right after."

"Don't leave town permanently," he said. "And if you could give me that address, I'd feel a lot better."

So, I did. I gave him the address to my old apartment, and Nico left. It was a weird feeling when all of the hubbub was over. You could almost feel it in the air that something major had happened, but when the sheriff and his deputies were gone, and the coroner had taken George's body, there was no evidence left that anything had gone on that morning.

Except that when I turned to go back into the house, George Cadell was sitting in a chair on the front porch. "What?" I whispered to myself.

Why would the coroner prop his body up in a chair and leave it like that? That didn't make any sense anyway. I'd seen him put George in a body bag, load him onto a gurney, and take him away in a van. I'd witnessed the entire thing.

And yet... There was George sitting on the porch staring at me.

The sun broke out from behind a fluffy white cloud and flooded the front porch with light. It was then that I could see he was transparent.

Just like the woman the night before. The one that I'd convinced myself had been a dream.

I looked around to see if anyone else was seeing what I was seeing, but no one was around. I had no idea what to do.

There was a ghost on my porch. Was I supposed to go talk to him? Should I walk around to the side door and avoid the specter all together?

"He's not real," I said to myself. "What you need is a psychiatrist."

I'd heard that when someone had delusions, you should not indulge them. I interpreted that advice as to apply to my own hallucinations and made my way quickly around to the house's side door. Better to just avoid it until I had some professional help.

When I got back in the house, Rook was in the kitchen making a sandwich. I'd had breakfast before I discovered George, but I found myself envious of his impending sandwich. Also, a little confused...

"Where did you get ham?" I asked. "And cheddar? Is that cheddar?"

"I thought you bought them at the store," he said.

"I didn't buy ham and cheddar," I said.

"Well, obviously, you did," he replied. "Would you like a mystery ham and cheese sandwich?"

That lightened the mood considerably until I realized it meant that I'd purchased groceries without knowing it. How long had I been walking around hallucinating? Was Rook even real? There was one way to find out.

"Sure, I'll take a sandwich. Can you toast the bread for mine first?" I asked.

"I suppose," he said completely deadpan.

I got a glass of Coke for each of us and then sat down at the kitchen table while Rook finished our sandwiches. It was the second time he'd prepared food for us. I figured I should handle dinner that evening even if it was ordering pizza.

Was there any place to get pizza in Fullmourn?

I was about to ask Rook when George appeared in the chair across from mine. He stared at me from the other side of the table.

Rook turned around with the two plates in his hand. They had the ham sandwiches, cut into triangles, and a huge pile of chips. He walked over and set one of the plates in front of me and the other in front of George. I kept looking from the ghost to my cousin and back again, but he didn't seem to see him.

"I need to run up to my room and get my phone," Rook said. "I feel weird without it. You can start without me. I won't be hurt."

"Rook…" I said, but my voice trailed off as I watched George in horror. He was trying, and failing, to pick up Rook's sandwich.

"Yeah?" Rook asked with one eyebrow cocked up in confusion.

"Hurry back," I said.

"I will," he confirmed. "Like I said, you don't have to wait for me." That last part he said over his shoulder as he left the kitchen.

When I turned back to George's ghost, he'd stopped trying to pick up the sandwich and had moved on to staring daggers into me. "Can you see me?" he asked.

"I can," I said. "But I shouldn't be talking to you."

"Why not?" he asked.

"Because you're a hallucination, and I'm sure it's not good for mental health to pretend like you're real," I said.

"I am not a hallucination," he said indignantly.

"You are," I said, "and the sudden onset of these symptoms has me worried. What if it's not mental illness? What if I have a brain tumor or something?"

"I'm not a hallucination or a symptom of a brain tumor," George said angrily. Things were not going well.

"I'm sorry," I said. "Okay, then what are you doing here?"

I had been working with the dead my entire adult life, and I'd never once encountered something overtly paranormal. Sure there had been little things like footsteps down an empty hall or a creaky morgue door, but those things could all technically be explained away.

So, I could not believe that George was real. Death was the final step in our life's journey, right? That's why it deserved so much respect and care.

"I'm going to sue you," George's voice broke me out of my reverie.

"I'm sorry, what?" I asked.

"If you don't figure out what is going on here, I'm going to sue you. What the heck happened to me? Why can I see through my hands?" George asked as he held his ghostly hands out in front of him and wiggled his fingers.

"I think you have a fundamental misunderstanding of what's going on here," I said.

"I am NOT a hallucination!" George said and sprung to his feet.

"Okay, well, even if I give you that... then you're a ghost. You can't sue me," I said.

"Who are you talking to?" Rook asked from behind me before George could say anything else.

When I turned back around, George was gone. "I was thinking of starting a novel," I blurted out. "I was just running over some dialogue. I like to think out loud."

"You're not a writer," he said accusingly. He knew I was lying.

"I could be," I said.

"What was the last thing you wrote?" he asked.

"A report for the medical examiner at my last job," I admitted. "Fine, I'm lying. I was talking to the ghost of George Cadell." Why couldn't I stop blurting things out? I really should have thought it over before telling Rook. "I've been seeing ghosts since after the funeral last night. I saw Annabelle too."

I was not going to tell him the part about the talking fairy mouse. That had to have been a dream.

"It's got to be the stress," Rook said as he took his seat at the table. "Have you ever talked to someone before?"

"I'm talking to you now," I said sarcastically.

"I mean a professional," he said before popping a chip in his mouth.

"No, I have never seen a psychiatrist," I said. "Maybe I should."

"I don't think it would hurt," Rook said. "If nothing else, maybe they can help you make the adjustment to your new life."

We finished eating in silence. When we were done, I washed the plates, and Rook dried.

"I need to do some things before we lose the rest of the day. I need a local bank account, and I'd like to go to my apartment and start planning my move," I said.

"Do you want me to go with you?" Rook asked.

"I think I can handle it," I said.

He looked a little disappointed. "I have that program I want to work on anyway."

"You can come with me if you want," I said.

"It's all right. I have a lot of work to do," Rook said and then left the kitchen.

I didn't have the chance to ask him where exactly the bank was located in Fullmourn, so I had to do a web search. I put the address in my phone and headed out for the second time that day.

When I almost had the front door open, I got a text. It was from Rook.

Can you check the mail on your way out? Or back in?

Sur,. I responded.

Without thinking about what I'd found the first time I went out the front door, I went that way again. At the bottom of the steps, something caught my eye.

The sun was hitting an object under the front porch. It was shiny and silver.

I got down on my knees and reached through the lattice. "Huh," I said to myself as I pulled the used scratch-off ticket out from the dark depths of the porch. "Looks like the local constabulary isn't that great at their jobs." I shoved the ticket into my purse and headed down the driveway to the mailbox.

It probably should have crossed my mind to call the sheriff, but I was focused on my errands. Distracted by everything else that was going on as well...

So, I just drove to the bank. It was housed in one of the newest buildings I'd seen in Fullmourn and had a large parking lot. I couldn't believe how many spaces there were, and exactly three of them were occupied.

The building's curving lines and huge row of floor-to-ceiling windows gave it a big-city feel. The perfectly manicured shrubbery reminded me of a Japanese garden. Whoever had designed the building and grounds had done so with a great deal of loving attention. It was completely out of place in Fullmourn, but then again, so was I.

When I went inside, there was what looked like one customer, one teller, and the bank manager. At least, I thought she was the bank manager. The woman was dressed in a sharp red suit and was milling around in the background behind the teller.

The customer seemed to be chatting it up with the teller, so I took my place in line. I half expected the manager lady to open another window, but after a couple of minutes, she looked at me and then disappeared into the back.

Figured.

I hated waiting in line for anything. It made me feel vulnerable in a way I couldn't quite put my finger on, so anytime I had to do it, I began feeling anxious and agitated. But, I waited a couple more minutes before I began clearing my throat.

"You heard that old goat George is dead," the customer said to the teller.

Wait a second... I decided it was a good time to practice a little patience.

"I did," the teller responded. Her nametag read Amelia. "It's all over town."

"Well, good riddance," the customer said.

"Janice, don't talk like that. Nobody liked George, but don't pretend you wanted him dead," Amelia said.

"Speak for yourself. That man was a blemish on our town," Janice said. "There's been more than a few times I wanted to wring his neck myself."

"People are going to think you did it," Amelia said, but her tone was teasing.

"Let them," Janice said completely deadpan. "Anyway, I've got to get going. Will wants roast for dinner, so I've got to get that going."

"Have a good day, Janice," Amelia said.

"You too," Janice returned. "Give my love to Bobby and the kids."

As Janice was leaving, she looked me over. I could have sworn I heard her grunt before continuing on her way. Guess she didn't like me either.

"How can I help you today?" Amelia asked.

I stepped up to the counter, got out my wallet, and began fishing around for my driver's license. "I'd like to open an account," I said. "I need a checking account with a debit card."

"I can certainly assist you with that. I'll need your social security number, two forms of identification, and I've got a brief form for you to fill out consenting to a credit check," she said with a genuine smile.

"Two forms of ID? Will my old employee badge do?" *Crap*, I thought. I hadn't actually quit my job. I wasn't going to be able to give them two weeks' notice either. Not living in Fullmourn. I hadn't really thought it all through. Perhaps I could commute, but what if I was on a shift at the hospital and Rook needed me? There were other technicians who could fill my shift until they hired someone. Rook didn't really have anyone else.

"Ma'am?" Amelia asked.

"Sorry. Yes. Did you say my work ID would be okay?" I shook my head as if trying to clear the cobwebs.

"As long as it has a photo," she said with a less enthusiastic smile.

Great. Now the teller at the bank thought I was nuts.

"Here you go," I said and slid the badge and my driver's license across the counter to her.

We did the rest of the paperwork, and I deposited the cash from the funeral into the bank. Thankfully, Fullmourn was up with the times, and Amelia was able to go into the back and make my debit card while I waited. The whole thing only took five extra minutes.

"Can I ask you one more thing before I go?" I ventured as she handed me my shiny new black debit card. I loved that they used black instead of blue.

"What can I help you with?"

"The woman who was in here before me, her name was Janice?" I asked.

"You mean Mrs. Badersmith?" Amelia asked.

"Yes," I said. "I wasn't sure if I recognized her or not. I'm new in town, and I'm trying to keep everybody straight."

"Yes, Mrs. Badersmith and her husband live over in the Sunny Hills Retirement Community," Amelia said.

"There are sunny hills around here?" I asked jokingly, but Amelia didn't laugh. She didn't seem to have a sense of humor about the rather gloomy, but I thought absolutely beautiful, weather in Fullmourn. "Anyway, is that a nursing home or something?"

"No. It's one of those active senior neighborhoods. You have to be over the age of fifty-five to live there. There's a recreation center and a pool. All that stuff. It's a relatively new neighborhood. They're still building quite a few houses. You're not in the market, are you?" Amelia asked.

"Me? No. I was just curious," I said.

"Yeah, because if you were fifty-five, I'd want to know what kind of witchcraft you practice," Amelia said. She cracked up at her own joke, and I felt compelled to chuckle along with her.

"Thank you so much," I said. "You have a good day."

With that, I left the bank prepared to head to my old apartment. I didn't really think that Janice Badersmith had killed George Cadel, but I filed her name and location away in my memory bank nonetheless.

Chapter Eight

On the drive back to my apartment, I managed to find the name and phone number of the only psychiatrist in Fullmourn. Since I had time and nothing to do but drive, I decided to give his office a ring.

"Dr. Peterson's office," a man said when he picked up the call.

"I guess I'm calling for Dr. Peterson," I said.

"Well, then this is your lucky day," the man said. "Speaking."

I was a little taken aback that he'd answered his own phone, but perhaps his practice was small enough that he didn't need a receptionist.

"I... Uh... I need an appointment," I said when I finally pulled my thoughts together. "I've just moved to Fullmourn, and I guess I'm having a little trouble adjusting."

"Oh, well, that's unfortunate to hear. Is this by chance the new funeral director?" he asked, and I should have known that he'd already know who I was.

"It is. My name is Hazel Holloway," I said.

"Well, thank you for calling me, Hazel. Is it all right if I call you Hazel? Or would you prefer Ms. Holloway?" Dr. Peterson asked.

"Hazel is fine," I said. "So, are you taking new patients?"

"I'm always willing to help my fellow Fullmournians. In fact, I could fit you in tonight at six?"

"Oh, really? You can get me in today?" I asked.

"Well, normally my last session ends at six, but I will stick around for you. We want you happy and well-adjusted in Fullmourn," he said and sounded very much like an infomercial.

"I appreciate that," I said. "Thank you."

"You are most welcome, Hazel. I will see you at six," he said.

As soon as we hung up, my phone beeped with a text message. I couldn't read it while I was driving, but I did see that it was from my work. The message was also marked as "important."

The reason the message was important became immediately clear. I read it as soon as I'd parked outside of my apartment and felt a sense of relief wash over me as soon as I was done.

I'd been laid off.

My boss had hoped that the message would reach me before I showed up for my next shift. Apparently, I wasn't going to get an in-person meeting over the matter or even a phone call. There was a brief explanation of budget cuts and Federal funding problems, but the decision was final. She hoped I had a good life and would give me an excellent reference.

It was like being dumped by Post-it note, but I wasn't sad. I actually felt kind of lucky. My problem had just sort of worked itself out.

There was a bit of a pep in my step as I crossed the parking area and walked into my building. The euphoric feeling died when I walked into my apartment.

I'd only spent one night at my new house, but it made my apartment feel like even more of a dump. Not that the place was filthy. I did a reasonably good job of keeping it tidy, but there was something else. It was a heaviness in the air, and I didn't realize it until I got away.

Suddenly, I had motivation to get my stuff packed and never, ever have to come back. I only had a few hours because I needed to be back in Fullmourn for my appointment with Dr. Peterson, but I got all of my stuff packed into boxes and booked a moving van.

It probably helped that I didn't have much to pack anyway. A combination of being broke plus not having all of the usual sentimental stuff meant that my entire life, minus my furniture, fit into a few boxes.

When it was all done, I got back on my phone and canceled the moving van. The boxes could fit in my car, and the furniture… Well, let's just say it wasn't worth paying to move it. I had far better at the funeral home.

With an hour left to go, I quickly took my bed apart and dragged it all down to the curb. Some guy saw me doing it and asked if he could have it. I told him he could if he helped me move the sofa and dining room table outside.

His eyes lit up when he went into my apartment and I told him he could have everything but the boxes.

Ten minutes later, a couple of his buddies pulled up in a pickup truck, and they cleaned the place out for me. All I had to do was carry my few boxes down to my car.

The drive back to Fullmourn was uneventful, and when I got there, I realized I still had plenty of time to drop off my boxes before my appointment with Dr. Peterson.

"Can you give me a hand with some boxes?" I walked into the kitchen and found Rook devouring some of the rotisserie chicken.

"Sure," he said before washing his hands and following me out to the driveway.

We carried them up to my bedroom and left them in the middle of the floor and around the edge of the bed. When we were done, I looked at the time.

"I've got to go," I said. "I've got an appointment with Dr. Peterson at six. He's squeezing me in."

"You really think it's that serious that you need to have an emergency session with a shrink?" Rook asked. He seemed genuinely concerned.

"I'm not sure, but I'd feel better if I could talk to someone. I mean a professional," I said. "Can you handle your own dinner? I'll just eat something when I'm done."

"Yes, Hazel. I was feeding myself before you got here," he said, and I could swear there was almost a chuckle. Almost.

"I know, but I mean something other than Coke and potato chips," I said.

"I'll be fine," he said. "Don't be a smother."

"You're right. Okay, well, I'm going to head out. I'll see you when I'm done," I said.

Rook went out ahead of me, and I followed him back downstairs. I was mostly out the back door when he went back to consuming the rotisserie chicken. I wasn't sure why I'd worried about him getting something to eat.

I found Dr. Peterson's location and parked on the street out in front of the beautiful Victorian that housed his office. There was a podiatrist in the building on the left and a hair salon on the right. The entire block was a lovely commercial area.

Right inside the front door of Dr. Peterson's office was a seating area in what had been the house's formal parlor. I wasn't sure if I should sit or stand, so I just stood awkwardly in the middle of the room. There was no receptionist, and I assumed I should just wait for the doctor.

I was only waiting for a couple of minutes when two men emerged from a hallway off the parlor. "I will see you next week," a man in black-framed glasses and a red sweater said to the other man. I didn't get a good look at him because when he saw me, he hurried out of the house. He'd been wearing a blue and green plaid shirt and jeans, but I hadn't seen enough of his face that I could identify him later. My guess was he didn't want me, or maybe anyone, knowing he was seeing Dr. Peterson.

"Ms. Holloway?" The man in the red sweater asked me as soon as the other was gone.

"That's me," I said.

"I'm Dr. Peterson," he said and extended his hand to me. "It's a pleasure to meet you."

"Thank you for seeing me on such short notice," I said and shook his hand.

"Would you follow me back to my office?" he asked and then waved me down the hallways.

His office was painted in a drab olive green with a dark wood chair rail that ran all the way around the room. It looked like a formal dining room that had been converted to an office. There was even a crystal chandelier that hung in the middle of the room.

"Have a seat," he said as we stepped into the office. "You can take the sofa or one of the chairs. It's up to you."

There were two wingback chairs covered in dark brown fabric and a matching sofa. I choose one of the chairs, and Dr. Peterson quickly sat down in the other.

"I record my sessions, so I don't have to take notes," he said and pulled out a small recorder. "I hope that's okay? If not, I can take notes, but I don't feel like you'd be getting my best that way."

"Will anyone else hear them?" I asked.

"Never," Dr. Peterson said with a reassuring smile. "I keep them locked in a cabinet. I'm the only one with a key, and if you ever choose to stop being a patient, then I can destroy them. That's at your request, of course."

"I don't mind then," I said.

"Good. Well, let's get started, then," he said and placed the recorder on his lap. "Why don't you tell me why you are here."

"Well..." I said and told him everything that I could recall from the last couple of days.

When I was finished with my story, Dr. Peterson clicked the stop button on his recorder. "So, you've seen the ghost of George Cadell as well?"

"Yes. After I found his body, I saw him at my kitchen table. That's when he threatened to sue me if I didn't solve his murder."

"Did he tell you anything else?" Dr. Peterson asked. "Like, did he give you any clue as to who killed him?"

"No, why?" I asked.

"Because it's fascinating," he said.

"The part about me being a witch isn't?" I asked. "I would have thought George's portion of the story would have been the least interesting."

"I believe that you're experiencing what is known as hypnagogia," Dr. Peterson said.

"That sounds horrible," I responded.

"It's a sleep condition. Basically, your brain stays in sleep mode even though you are mostly conscious. So, you have waking dreams that can be quite frightening," Dr. Peterson said.

"So, you don't think I have schizophrenia?" I asked.

"At this time, I would not make that diagnosis. What I do think you have is depression and possibly anxiety. That's what's causing you to have the hypnagogia episodes. I believe that if we can bring those conditions under control, not only will you feel better, but the episodes will stop," he said.

"How do we do that?" I asked.

"I'm going to write you a prescription for a beta blocker for the anxiety. It will help keep your heart rate under control. It will basically take away any physical signs of anxiety and give your brain some space. Anxiety tends to be a loop. Plus, I'd like you to take an antidepressant. Just something mild. Also, a mild antipsychotic."

"You said I wasn't schizophrenic," I protested.

"Don't let the name scare you. Most antipsychotics also work as mood stabilizers. Since you are having some hallucinations, I think it's appropriate," he said.

"That's a lot of medication," I said.

"I want you to feel better quickly," Dr. Peterson said. "My aim is to ensure that you can successfully fulfil your new duties."

"Okay," I said. I was still hesitant, but I did want to stop having hallucinations. He was a doctor, and I'd gone to him for help, so I figured I should at least give it a try.

"Good," he said. "I'll give you the prescriptions, and you can go to the pharmacy at the square and have them filled. They should have all of these medications in stock, so you can get started on your new regimen right away."

I waited as he filled out three separate prescriptions from a pad he'd pulled out of his desk drawer. It had been a long time since I'd seen a doctor use actual paper prescriptions. I'd long gotten used to them doing it all on the computer, but things in small towns were different.

"You're sure about this?" I asked as I took the scripts from him.

"Absolutely, and if it doesn't work out, we can discuss that at your med check in a month," he said. "Same time one month from today work for you?"

"Wait, I'm not going to see you again for a month? What about therapy? I figured we'd meet at least weekly and talk," I said.

"I don't really have room in my schedule for another talk therapy patient, Hazel. But, I can do your medication management. If you need a psychologist, then I can coordinate with them," he said.

"Is there a psychologist in Fullmourn?" I asked. "I didn't see anything when I was googling it."

"No, you'll either have to go to someone in a nearby town, or there are excellent online options," he said. "If you'd like, I can help you select one."

"That's okay," I said. "Thank you for seeing me on such short notice."

"Just remember to take your meds. You'll be right as rain in no time at all," Dr. Peterson said with a huge smile.

I left the office feeling a bit bewildered, and I hadn't been expecting Dr. Peterson to be such a huge believer in pharmaceutical therapy.

"You're just being silly," I told myself once I was back in my car. "You can't actually expect things to be like they are on television."

It was the truth, though. My only experience with therapy was watching it happen on television and in movies. My expectation had been that I'd lie on a sofa and tell him all my troubles after which Dr. Peterson would tell me how to deal with those issues. My expectations had been incorrect.

I thought about not filling the prescriptions and just driving straight back to the funeral home, but something inside of me just knew that if I did that, I'd find George Cadell and a talking fairy mouse waiting for me. If I wanted to get rid of them, I had to take the pills.

"You're not nuts," I told myself as I parked my car in front of the pharmacy at the square. "Almost everyone needs a little help from time to time. It's not shocking that you didn't come out right given your upbringing... or the fact that you're sitting in front of a pharmacy talking to yourself about your prescriptions for crazy pills."

At that point, I stopped talking to myself and got out of the car. Edwards Pharmacy was an inviting place. It reminded me of another era. One I'd only seen... in the movies.

There was soft, vaguely '50s sounding, music playing over the PA system when I walked in. The air was warm but not stifling, and the store smelled like fruity ice cream and grilled burgers. Probably because on one side of the store, there was an old-fashioned soda counter serving various ice cream treats, burgers, and hot dogs. I couldn't resist. On my way to the actual pharmacist's counter in the back, I stopped and put in an order for two burgers, homemade chips, and two fountain vanilla Cokes.

"I'll be back in a few minutes to pick it up, if that's okay?" I said to the woman behind the counter.

"Take your time, and I'll bag it up. Unless that's all for you?" She eyed me shrewdly up and down.

"Nope, I'm sharing," I said.

"No judgment," she responded. "I was just going to be very jealous if you could eat all that and keep your figure."

"Don't I wish," I said with a chuckle.

"Don't we all, honey," she said and set to work putting the burger patties on the small grill.

I made my way to the back of the store and waited at the drop-off window. Eventually, a tall, elderly man with fluffy white hair and an even whiter coat appeared on the other side.

"How can I help you?" He wore a nametag that said "Harold" and "Pharmacist."

"I have these to fill," I said and slid the prescriptions across the counter for him.

"Dr. Peterson," he said as he picked them up and read them.

There was something in his tone that I couldn't quite place. Perhaps it was a hint of disdain, but I didn't know if that was for me or for Dr. Peterson. I wasn't going to ask.

"Yes," I said. "Is there a problem? He said you would have these medications. I can go to another pharmacy if you don't."

"No need for that. I've got plenty of them. Even if I didn't, I could order them for you," he said with a soft smile.

"Good to know," I said.

"Give me about five to ten minutes," he said.

While I waited for my new meds, I wandered around the pharmacy. There were a couple of people who'd come in and taken a spot at the soda counter. Otherwise, there was just one other person in the store.

I was perusing mascara when she walked into the aisle on the other side of mine. Since the shelves didn't go all the way to the ceiling, I could hear her talking on her phone.

"You know," she said and cleared her throat, "I always said that George Cadell jerk was going to end up dead."

This piqued my interest, so I tried to move in a little closer without knocking the shelf over.

"Don't tell me you don't think he deserved it?" she continued. "I think whoever killed him did this town a service. Last week he poisoned his neighbor's lawn." There was a pause. "No, his lawn. Not his dog. If George had killed a dog, I imagine he would have been strung up in the town square. Don't you remember a huge portion of his neighbor Max's lawn was poisoned... Yes, I'm sure it was George. Think about it. Who else would it be?"

After that, she wandered off and I couldn't hear the conversation anymore. My choice was to either let it go or try to follow her.

Trailing after her to try and hear more sounded a bit stalkery, so I went back to shopping for mascara. The selection was slim, but they had Maybelline Blackest Black, and that was the godmother of goth girls' mascara. I'd loved that stuff since junior high. My bottle at home was mostly empty, so I grabbed a package off the display and headed back to the pick-up counter.

"Ah, you're just in time," Harold said. "Would you like me to ring that up with your medications? Or you can take it up front?"

"If you don't mind," I said and slid it across the counter to him.

"I don't at all. Do you have any insurance you'd like me to bill?" he asked.

I hadn't thought about that. I didn't have any insurance anymore because I'd been laid off from my job. Not that the policy I had through them was worth much. I'd have to remember to sign up for a personal plan, but for the time being, I'd need to pay cash for the pills.

"I don't," I said. "Cash, I guess."

"You sure?" he asked.

"They're expensive, aren't they?" I cringed because I knew how pricy prescription drugs could be without insurance.

"Two of them aren't because they're older and the generics are in the ten-dollar program. The third one is $600 per month," he said. "Unless Dr. Peterson increases your dose, and then we're looking at $750."

I took a deep breath. That was steep, but I could afford it. "It's fine," I said. "I'll pay cash now and work on getting a private insurance policy."

"I'm sure Rook has something. You should ask him who he uses," Harold said.

It hadn't occurred to me until that moment that he knew exactly who I was. Everyone already knew me before I met them, and now

Harold, the pharmacist, knew I'd been prescribed antipsychotics less than a week after arriving. I knew I shouldn't have felt embarrassed, but I couldn't help feeling a little self-conscious.

"That's a good idea," I said. "It was nice to meet you, Harold. I'm Hazel, by the way, but it seems you already knew that."

"Your name's on the prescriptions," he said with a chuckle.

"Oh, right." I could be such a dolt sometimes.

"But you're right, I would have known anyway. Welcome to small-town living," he said. "And welcome to Fullmourn. You must be very special if your great-uncle chose you to take over his business. So, do you have any questions about the medications? Directions for taking them are on the labels and the attached instruction sheets."

"I don't because I don't know enough about them to even know what to ask," I said.

He blew a short breath out through his nose. "Dr. Peterson didn't go over that with you?"

"No, not really, but he did fit me in at the last minute. I think he was short on time," I said though I had no earthly idea why I was defending Dr. Peterson.

Harold took a few minutes to go over the pills with me. He told me which ones I should take with food and explained how I could use the beta blocker as needed instead of taking it regularly. Dr. Peterson also left out that I'd need to monitor my heart rate if I did take it to ensure it didn't go too low.

"Thank you," I said when Harold was done with his review.

"If you think of questions later, you can always call or email," he said and slid a card across the counter to me. "If it's too early or late to call the pharmacy, then send me an email. I'll get back to you as soon as I can."

"Thank you so much," I said again, and I walked away from the pharmacy counter feeling a little more confident about taking the meds Dr. Peterson had prescribed.

On my way out, I stopped by the soda fountain and picked up my dinner order. I hoped that Rook hadn't eaten an entire bag of chips waiting for me to come home because the burgers and fries smelled amazing.

I drove home quickly so we could both eat while it was still hot. "Dinner," I called out as I walked into the back door of the funeral home. "Come and get it!"

Except that if Rook was on the top floor, there was no way he would hear me. He didn't. I had to take out my phone and text him to come downstairs for food.

While I waited, I started unpacking the food and setting the table. When I turned around after grabbing plates from the cabinet, the little fairy mouse was there in the middle of the kitchen floor. His tiny wings unfurled in a gorgeous display of ethereal rainbow light.

"We need to talk," he said and wiggled his little nose.

I dropped the plates.

"What was that?" I heard Rook call from out in the hallway.

I instinctively turned toward the sound of his voice, and when I looked back, the mouse was gone. "I dropped the plates," I said as Rook walked into the kitchen.

"You all right?" Rook asked.

"Yeah, I just need to start the medicine Dr. Peterson gave me sooner rather than later. I'll do it as soon as we eat," I said.

"You're taking medication?" Rook's face wrinkled with concern.

"Yep. Dr. Peterson said it would be best," I responded.

"What do you say?" Rook asked.

"I say that I want to be able to do my job here and not let you or our clients down," I said. "I'll try the medication and see."

Rook looked like he wanted to say more, but he sat down and started eating instead. "Thanks for this," he said in between bites.

"You're welcome. Do you like it?" I asked.

"It's from the soda fountain at the pharmacy, right? I love their food, but I never go in there."

"Well, now I have a reason to go in once a month," I said.

"We'll see," Rook said. "Let's just see how you take to whatever Dr. Peterson prescribed."

After dinner I took the pills and went upstairs to my room. Before I did, Rook said he had to meet with a family the next morning, so he was going to turn in early too.

"Don't you need me for that?" I asked.

"Not for this one," he said.

"Why? What did I do?" I asked. "Is it because of the meds? Are you doubting me?"

"No, it's because it's George Cadell's family," Rook said. "I'll handle the arrangements for this."

"They're coming here?" I asked. "They want us to do his funeral?"

"No. They don't want us to do it, but we're the only funeral home available. So, it's sort of more of a have to thing."

"Oh," I responded. "Do they think I killed him?"

"Just let me handle all of it, okay?" Rook asked. "Please trust me."

"Of course," I said. "Good night, Rook."

"Night, Hazel," Rook said.

After I brushed my teeth and put on my pajamas, I was getting ready to get into bed when I got a text message. I figured it was

Rook, but it wasn't, and at first I couldn't figure out who it could be.

I need to meet with you about George Cadell's death tomorrow. The text said.

It took me a couple of minutes to figure it out, but eventually it dawned on me that it was the sheriff. Nico needed to meet with me about the murder.

That couldn't be good.

Chapter Nine

I was in the kitchen making coffee the next morning when I got a text from Nico asking me to come outside. It seemed a bit strange, but sure enough, when I looked out the kitchen window, his cruiser was in the driveway.

"How long have you been here?" I asked the empty kitchen.

Well, at least I'd thought it was empty. "Who are you talking to?" Rook asked from behind me.

I jumped and dropped the coffee mug, but fortunately, he caught it. "Don't need you breaking any more of these," he said.

"It's a good thing there's no coffee in there," I said.

"That's very true," Rook handed the mug back to me. "Anyway, who are you talking to?"

"Oh, I just got a text from Nico. He wants me to come outside. I got another text from him last night saying he needed to talk to me today. I was mostly talking to myself, but I was kinda wondering how long he'd been here," I said.

"Well, he's probably outside in the solace garden," Rook said. "He's out there a lot, actually."

"The solace garden?" I asked.

"Out the back door, across the driveway, and through the fancy iron gate. It's on the left," Rook said.

"I should take him some coffee," I said.

"I'm sure he would appreciate that," Rook confirmed. "I'm going to make some toast. You want me to make you any?"

"No, thanks. I'll get some when I come back in. You've got the meeting with George Cadell's family, and I'll need something to keep me busy."

"Don't worry, I'll fill you in on everything," Rook said as he popped two slices of the bread into the toaster.

"You better."

I poured two cups of coffee, and Rook held the back door for me as I went outside. "Need help with that gate?" he asked.

"I think I can get it," I said.

I had to set my cup down in the grass to get the gate open, but I did manage to finagle my way through without spilling either cup. Once inside, the garden took my breath away.

It was a most extraordinary surprise. The layout consisted of concentric circles of alternating stone path and green space. There was one main path that cut through it all and went to the center circle.

Nico sat on one of the three benches surrounded by what looked like exotic flowers and plants. I couldn't quite put my finger on it, but the flora was both exotic and familiar at the same time. More than mere roses and geraniums comprised the garden. There were lilacs, though, and they smelled heavenly.

"I hope black is okay?" I asked when Nico looked up at me. "If not, I can go back inside for cream and sugar."

"If I didn't know any better, I'd have sworn you were an angel," he said.

"Sorry?"

"Black is fine," he said with a chuckle. "Thank you for bringing me coffee. The stuff at the station is a joke."

"You know, you're the sheriff, right? You could change that," I said.

"Well, then I wouldn't have a built-in excuse to go to Mugs every day," he said.

"Mugs?" I asked.

"Mugs Coffee Shop. It's the coffee house on the square. Right next door to the Frost Goddess Bakery," he said.

"Oh, yeah. I remember seeing them both. Any good?" I asked.

"They are both amazing," Nico said. "The best coffee and..."

"Donuts?" I blurted out and instantly regretted it.

"I was going to say cinnamon rolls. They make them fresh every day, and the cream cheese icing is to die for. Or you can get them with a pecan glaze if icing isn't you're thing. There's a maple bacon cupcake that's amazing as well, but I'll deny it if you ever tell anyone I eat them," Nico said.

"Is there problem with liking maple bacon cupcakes?" I asked.

"It's seen as rather exotic around here," Nico said. "People prefer to see their sheriff as a little more traditional."

"That's some intense scrutiny," I said. "I can't imagine."

"You'll get used to it. You'd be amazed what passes for a scandal around here," Nico said.

"I'm sure that George's murder has stirred people up, then," I said and took a sip of my coffee.

"Speaking of which, that's why I'm here," Nico said.

"I figured. How can I help?" I asked.

"I wanted to see if you remembered anything else about that day?" Nico said. "I'd like to mark you off my suspect list if possible. So, can you tell me anything that will help me do that?"

"I'm officially a suspect?" I asked.

"I'm not going to arrest you or anything like that right now, but I'd rather just move on to someone else," he said.

"I don't remember anything else..." I remembered the lottery scratcher I'd found under the front porch. I'd tucked it into the pocket of my jeans before coming downstairs that morning. "I did find this," I said and pulled the ticket out of my pocket. "I found it under the front porch yesterday when I was leaving."

Nico didn't take the ticket. "Hold that thought," he said and stood up.

I watched as he walked out of the solace garden. He was gone for a couple of minutes while I just sat there holding the ticket out in front of me like an idiot. Eventually, Nico returned with a plastic bag.

"Drop it in there if you don't mind," he said.

"Is that an evidence bag?" I asked.

"It is. I don't want to contaminate it any more than you already have," he said gruffly.

"I'm sorry," I retorted. "I've been out of sorts."

"You should have called me when you found that," he said sternly.

"I'm realizing that now. Again, I'm sorry," I said.

"Wasn't your altercation with George at the gas station over these tickets?" Nico asked.

"It was, but it wasn't an altercation. He was being a jerk," I said.

"Still doesn't look good for you," Nico said.

"If I thought for a second that ticket was evidence against me, then why would I just hand it over to you? You and your deputies didn't find it. I could have just hidden it or destroyed it," I said.

"That's a fair point," Nico admitted. "Didn't you say there was another man at the gas station that had words with George?"

"There was. He was the one who ultimately got George to get out of the line, but I don't know who he was. He did look like a trucker," I said.

"Well, I can go to the gas station and review the security footage," Nico said.

"Do you really think that guy killed George?" I asked.

"I don't know who killed George, but I'm going to find out," Nico said and stood up. "Charlie never minded if I sat out here as long as there wasn't a funeral going on. What about you?"

"I don't mind at all," I said. "Can I ask why you like it here so much? Aren't there any other parks in Fullmourn?"

"It's quiet here," he said. "And my wife is here."

"I'm sorry... what do you mean?" I asked.

"My wife's ashes are buried here," he said and pointed to a large shrub with white flowers blooming from its vine-like branches. "She's buried under that plant because it was her favorite. My wife passed when we were young, but she helped design and plant this garden. So she's here in more ways than one. But mostly it's quiet, and I come here to think. She's been gone for quite some time, and I've moved past it. Mostly because that's what she'd have wanted."

"I'm so sorry," I said.

"No reason to be. Like I said, it's been a long time. We were pretty much kids when we got married in the first place. I'm grateful for the time I got to spend with her. My grieving has passed."

"That's an excellent way to view things," I said because I wasn't sure what else to say.

"I should go," Nico said. "I'll contact you when I need to speak to you again."

I bid him farewell and stayed in the garden for a few minutes alone. There was something about Nico's wife's favorite plant that I just couldn't put my finger on at first. It looked a lot like a moonflower, but it couldn't be that. The blooms were out in full even in the morning sun.

Datura.

It was a datura plant. Also known as jimsonweed, thornapples, and the devil's trumpet.

Or hell's bells.

Nico's wife's favorite plant was poison and also hallucinogenic. It depended on the dose.

As I looked around, it hit me what had been off about the garden. They were all deadly. The solace garden was a poisoner's garden.

There was also angel's trumpet. It was an amazing aphrodisiac right before it killed you. The death was painless.

Laurel hedge lined the outer wall of the garden, and within I found foxglove, black hellebore, monkshood, and the gorgeous black berries of the belladonna.

Beautiful but lethal.

Had Nico's wife been some sort of witch? Maybe a serial killer?

Both options seemed completely ridiculous, but if I'd learned anything working for the medical examiner, it was to not discount people's capacity to surprise you. Either way, we needed to put a sign on the gate. Maybe Charlie and Rook didn't mind letting people just waltz into a garden full of toxic plants, but I would at least warn them.

Chapter Ten

The solace garden was beautiful, and it gave me the strong urge to come back after dark and see it at night. I couldn't linger any longer, though, because I heard a couple of cars pull up in the driveway.

George's family had arrived for their consultation with Rook, and while I couldn't be in the consultation, it was my funeral home. I fully intended to find an inconspicuous spot to hang out and listen.

When you take George's family into the office, leave the door open. I fully intend to eavesdrop. I sent the text to Rook.

? Was the text I got back.

Just do it. Please. I returned.

Whatever you say, boss lady.

I was tempted to call him on that, but I needed to let him do his job. I could hear the family making their way up the front walk, and as soon as they were clear of the driveway, I was going to head inside through the side door.

When it was clear, I went inside and put Nico's coffee cup in the sink. I got myself another cup and waited in a dark hallway for Rook to take the family into the office.

Once the coast was clear, I tiptoed out from my shadowy corner. Rook had left the office door open a few inches, and I could hear voices coming from inside. I couldn't understand exactly what they were saying, so I got closer.

I stood outside the door, mostly out of sight unless someone came out of the room and walked right into me, and sipped my coffee. Rook sounded like an entirely different person when he was dealing with the family.

There was an edge of confidence and authority that I'd never heard in his voice. "So, we'll go over your casket options first, and then I'll help you through more details after that. My aim is to make this entire process as comfortable as possible."

"We don't need to go over options," a woman said. "We're only here because my brother's will stipulates that we have to have a large funeral for him or we inherit nothing. Large doesn't mean expensive, though. We want whatever is cheapest."

Well, that was interesting...

"I see," Rook said. "Well, just for your own edification, even our least expensive options are quite lovely."

"We really don't care," a man's voice said. "I am a little concerned that the new funeral director has it in for my family, so can we hurry this along?"

That was me. He was talking about me. I took another sip of my coffee.

"Okay, well, if you folks will sit tight, I'll finalize the paperwork for you to sign. Do you have any color preferences? What kind of wood do you want for the casket? Even at our most economical price point, there are choices. What about flowers? And how many seats do you want in the viewing room?"

"The funeral needs to take place at the Fullmourn Cemetery. We won't need a viewing here," George's sister said. "Otherwise, we don't care about colors or wood choices. You've probably done this a million times, so can you just throw something together."

"I can," Rook said. I listened as his fingers began flying across the keyboard. There was an urgency to his typing that told me he wanted to get out of there as soon as possible.

"Claudia, don't you think it's just a little disrespectful to let the funeral director choose everything? We're inheriting his estate, so maybe we should put just a little bit of thought into it," the man said.

"With all due respect, Kurt, shut up," she snapped.

I heard the man snort. Rook let out a little gasp.

"You always do this," Kurt said. "You can't even fake being a decent human for one day."

Oh, boy.

"Folks, I can plan everything. This is a difficult time, and it's okay if you want to step out for a breather," Rook said.

"Now you want to kick us out?" Kurt said indignantly.

"Of course he does, Kurt, you're acting like a caveman," Claudia said.

"I've had about enough of you," Kurt said.

"Feeling's mutual, brother," Claudia spat back. "You know, this is why George forced us to throw him a funeral to get the inheritance. He hated me because I was mom and dad's favorite, and he knew you would act like a petulant child. He knew we would get into it. He's probably watching from heaven laughing hysterically at us."

"More like from Hell," Kurt said, but I heard him stand up and push his chair back.

"More like from the hallway," a voice from behind me made me jump and almost drop my coffee. If it hadn't been three-quarters empty, I'd have sloshed it all over my feet and the carpet.

I turned around and found myself face to face with George's ghost. Or rather, my hallucination of George's ghost. He had a huge, satisfied smile plastered on his face.

"Go away," I whispered.

I closed my eyes and prayed that when I opened them, he would be gone. He was not.

"I'll go away when you figure out who killed me. Until then, I'm going to enjoy my family's misery. That's all they ever gave me, after all," George said.

154

I shuffled down the hall when George's brother and sister came out of my office. They both gave me a dirty look but proceeded to bicker as they walked out the front door of the funeral home. George's ghost trailed off behind them. By the time Rook emerged from the office, all three Cadell siblings, both alive and dead, had moved on.

"Wow," I said to Rook when he looked at me with wide, glassy eyes.

"It's not the worst I've ever seen," he said. "You want to come in here, and I'll show you how to do all of the arrangements? We'll get everything ordered and arranged for three days from now."

"Three days?" I asked as I followed him back into the office.

"Yeah, we've got to get the casket ordered, contact the florist, and the Fullmourn Cemetery will need that much notice to get things set up," Rook said.

"Let's do it, then," I said.

I tried to follow along with everything Rook showed me, but I couldn't help watching the door for George's ghost.

Chapter Eleven

Three days later...

The morning of George Cadell's funeral, I woke up with a pounding headache and a sour stomach. I'd never been a big drinker, so that morning was worse than any hangover I'd ever suffered.

I went into my bathroom and drank a glass of water, hoping that I was just dehydrated. It did make me feel a little more awake and a little less queasy, so I figured it was all the salt in my diet. See, I wasn't actually hungover. Rook and I hadn't gone on a bender the night before. He'd gone up to his room to work on his project, and I'd fallen asleep in bed reading.

Despite feeling like utter garbage, I could say one positive thing. I hadn't seen a ghost of that fairy mouse the entire three days. If the pills were making me sick, I'd just have to adjust because they'd cleared my hallucinations right up. I didn't even know those types of medications could work that fast, but I convinced myself they had.

One thing I had done in the prior three days was get myself some proper black dresses and skirt suits for conducting funerals. I chose a black jacket and smart-looking pencil skirt from my closet and headed off for the shower.

Rook would be conducting George's funeral, but I was going along to help. I figured I'd help him get everything set up, and then I'd hang back and stay out of sight.

If nothing else, there was a gigantic cemetery for me to explore. I used to spend hours in cemeteries when I was a teen. I'd take photographs and do gravestone rubbings until it got too dark to see. So, I was a bit excited about the prospect of spending some time in the famous Fullmourn Cemetery.

The first task of the morning, after breakfast, was to help Rook load the casket into the hearse. Fortunately, the cart that he used to bring the caskets up from the basement had a motorized lift on it, so we basically just had to gently shove it into the back.

"How are we going to get the casket from the hearse to the grave without the cart?" I asked as Rook closed the car's back door.

"Pallbearers," Rook said. "If the family doesn't have six, then we can help. If that's still not enough, we can find volunteers or hire someone."

"That's sad," I said, "to have to hire someone to do that."

"Fortunately, it rarely happens," Rook said. "Even George has enough family to do the job. They'll meet us there."

Rook drove the hearse, and I looked out the window as we made our way from the funeral home to the cemetery. I spaced out, but when we pulled through the gates, I couldn't believe my eyes.

"Is this really it?" I asked Rook and straightened up in my seat.

"It is," he said. "It's not famous for no reason."

"I can't see the other side," I said. "It goes all the way to the horizon."

"That it does," he answered as we drove down one of the cemetery roads towards a large blue tent. "And beyond."

"I can't believe I've never heard of this before," I said.

"I can't either," Rook answered, but before we could discuss it further, we were at the funeral site.

George's pallbearers were there waiting for us, so I made myself scarce. Strangely, though, I don't remember much.

I walked around the cemetery for what felt like a few minutes, so Rook tapping me on my shoulder and asking if I was ready to go took me by surprise.

"Already?" I asked. "That must have been the fastest funeral in history."

"What are you talking about?" Rook looked perplexed. "It's been at least two hours. The service has been over for about forty-five minutes. I've been looking for you. Why didn't you answer your phone, Hazel?"

"My phone didn't ring," I said, but when I went to take it out of my purse, it wasn't there. "I don't have my phone. My purse fell over when we were driving here. I bet it's on the floor. I'm so sorry."

"Are you okay?" Rook asked.

"I think so, why?" I asked, but come to think of it, I didn't feel that great.

"You look pale and your eyes are all glassy. Have you been drinking?" Rook asked.

"No. It's weird because I felt hungover this morning, but I haven't had a drink since right before the old woman's funeral," I said.

"Hazel?" Rook asked.

"Yeah?" I countered.

"You're sitting down," he said.

"What do you mean?" But I looked, and I had plopped down on the ground. One leg was sticking straight out while the other was bent because I was dressed in the pencil skirt suit. "Oh. When did that happen?"

"Just now," he said. "You just sat down. Let me help you up."

"That would be great," I said and thrust my arms out towards him like a toddler demanding to be picked up.

"I would laugh at you if I wasn't so worried," Rook said. Concern lined his face.

"I'm okay," I said, but the words were cut off by a loud, nasty belch.

"Are you going to be sick?" Rook asked. He'd pulled me halfway up from the ground and looked like he was ready to drop me.

"I don't feel so great," I said.

"Are you going to puke right now?" he asked sternly.

"No, but I'm lightheaded and my stomach is churning," I said. "I need to get home and lie down."

"Can you stand?" Rook asked as I realized that he still had me dangling by the hands half off the ground.

"I would have said yes until I realized the predicament I'm currently in," I said.

Next thing I knew, Rook's arms were hooked under mine and he was completely hoisting me up. "Just hold still, okay?" he asked as my feet lifted off the ground. "And please let me know if you're going to throw up."

"You can't pick me up," I protested as he picked me up. "I'm too heavy."

"You can't be a pound over 120," Rook said as he started walking back toward the car. Or, at least what I assumed was the direction of the car. "Remember that I shlep bodies much heavier than you around. I can handle you."

"It's not polite to guess a woman's weight like that," I protested softly.

"Am I wrong?" Rook asked as he took long, gentle steps that kept me from bouncing around too much.

"No. I fluctuate between one seventeen and one nineteen. I have since I was thirteen," I said. "I've tried to gain weight, but I have some gut issues. I've tried everything."

"Did Dr. Peterson discuss those issues with you when he prescribed those meds? Did he even look at your medical records?" Rook sounded annoyed.

"No," I said and sucked in a deep breath. All the talking was making me even more nauseated.

"You good?" Rook asked and stopped walking.

"I think so. I think I need to be quiet now," I said.

"I'm taking you to the hospital," Rook said.

"Uh-uh," I said and shook my head furiously. "I just need to lie down."

He thought about it for a few steps. "Fine, I'll take you home to lie down, but if you're not better in two hours, I'm taking you to the hospital."

"Deal," I whispered.

We passed the cemetery workers filling in the grave with a backhoe on the way to the car. Rook put me in gently and slowly drove out of the graveyard.

There was a difference between a cemetery and a graveyard, but I couldn't quite remember it. They seemed the same to me either way...

I rolled down the window and let my head hang halfway out. The breeze on my face felt good, and if I hurled, I wouldn't do it inside the car.

"It's a little out of the way, but I'm going to stop at the grocery store and get some ginger ale," Rook said. "You think you can make it a few extra minutes? I'd take you home first, but I don't want to leave you alone."

"I can make it," I mumbled. By that point, my head was still pounding, my stomach still felt like it was full of spoiled limes, but I was half asleep.

I didn't really remember Rook stopping at the store, but at some point, he handed me a cold bottle of ginger ale. There was no way I could drink it in the car, so I just pressed the cold plastic to my forehead.

It felt good.

Rook pulled into the driveway at Holloway and Sons. He parked the hearse by the side door and came around to get me.

The motion of him pulling me out of the car sent my stomach roiling. "I'm going to be sick," I said and tried to hold back.

Rook half carried and half dragged me into the bathroom. He held my hair back and pressed a cool washcloth to my face every time I came up for air.

Eventually, I was spent. "I think I can go lie down now," I said. "Can you help me to my room?"

Rook helped me upstairs and stood outside the bathroom door while I washed my face, brushed my teeth, and changed into pajamas. I sat on the edge of my bed and drank half of the ginger ale. My stomach was already better from throwing up, and the cool soda soothed it even more.

"I'm staying here for a while," Rook said after he tucked me into bed. "I need to keep an eye on you for a bit."

"Fine," I said. "If your creepy behind wants to watch me sleep, so be it."

I looked at his face, and he smiled a bit. "That's better," he said.

"I think it's the medicines doing this," I said in a moment of clarity. "I was fine until I started taking them. My stomach has been upset since the first dose."

"Have you been eating more than I've seen you eating?" Rook asked.

"No," I said. "But I had breakfast this morning. You were there."

"Hazel, you ate three-quarters of a piece of toast and half a strip of bacon," Rook said.

"I only half of one piece of bacon?" I asked.

"I thought it was very strange as well," Rook said. "You went to the store, got more food, and you've barely eaten any of it."

"But I haven't had any more hallucinations," I said. "Maybe it's worth it."

"You shouldn't be taking that stuff," Rook said flatly. "It's too much too soon. Plus, he put you on antipsychotics after saying you weren't suffering from a psychotic disorder."

"He said it also helps with serious mood disorders," I protested. "Besides, you're the one who suggested I see a shrink."

"One, I didn't think you would listen to me," Rook said. "And two, I guess I didn't think you'd see Dr. Peterson. He's a quack, and most people in this town know it."

"Who else would I see?" I asked.

"I don't know. I thought maybe you knew someone back in your old city. You worked at the hospital," Rook said.

"Yeah, I don't," I said.

"And you've never seen someone before for mental health issues?" Rook asked.

"Never needed to," I said.

"You have zero history of major mood disorders that would require an antipsychotic mediation?" Rook said.

"Pretty much," I responded. "My family has plenty of issues, though. Charlie seems to be the only one who escaped them."

"I've heard," Rook said. "Still, I don't think you need or should be taking all that medication."

"Is that your professional opinion?" I teased.

"It's my friend opinion," he said. "And don't make any dumb comments about us being friends. I don't want to hear it. Go to sleep."

"Yes, sir," I said but I was already drifting off.

When I woke up, I felt better. It was dark outside, so I must have slept all day and part of the evening too. Rook was gone. He must have stayed until he was sure I was okay and then went to his room or downstairs.

I wasn't hungry at all, but I knew I should eat. I also had to decide if I was going to keep taking the medicine or not. In that moment, I was more than inclined to drop them. Hallucinations or not, there was no way I could go through life feeling that horrible.

"Glad to see you upright," the little voice said from the middle of my bedroom floor.

I reached over and flicked on the bedside lamp.

He was there.

His little wings unfurled and his nose twitched. The tiny fairy mouse was back.

How was that possible? The medication was supposed to keep me from hallucinating. I hadn't seen him for days, but there he was back again. My heart sank. Feeling like crap was one thing but feeling so terrible and still hallucinating?

Was there no hope for me?

"I'm not a hallucination," the little mouse said. "My name is Loftus. I am Loftus with the Mostus."

"How do you know what I am thinking?" I asked but instantly realized what a dumb question I'd asked. "Of course you know what's in my head. You're my imagination."

"No," Loftus said. "I know what you're thinking because you've been talking about it with Rook."

"That makes sense. I guess you do live in the walls," I said. "No, wait. No. No. Absolutely not. You do not live in the walls. You have not been eavesdropping on my conversations with Rook. You aren't real. You're a hallucination."

"If that's true, then why am I here right now, Hazel? You've been dumping powerful medications down your throat for days. There's no way you're hallucinating."

"Dr. Peterson said it was a mild antipsychotic. Maybe it's just taking some time to work."

"Dr. Peterson lied to you, Hazel. There's nothing mild about those drugs or the doses. I don't know why he wanted you catatonic, but that's where you're headed if you keep taking them," Loftus said.

"You're lying," I said.

"Am I lying or am I a hallucination?" Loftus asked.

"You could be both," I countered. "One does not exclude the other."

"That's true," Loftus said. "There has to be a way for me to prove I'm real."

"I'm not sure if that's a good idea," I said.

"What? Why not?" Loftus asked. "Lady, maybe you really are a crazy person."

"I think that might be better," I said.

"If you're crazy?" Loftus asked.

"Yeah, because if you're real, then the world isn't what I think it is. I'm not sure if I'm ready for something like that. I've had a lot of changes lately," I said.

"You don't know the half of it," Loftus said.

"What?" Now it was my turn to be confused. Well, more confused.

"You're a witch now," Loftus said. "That's why you can hear me and see me in my true form."

"If I wasn't a witch, I wouldn't be able to see you?" I asked.

"No, you'd be able to see me. I'd just be a mouse," Loftus said. "Boring."

"I think I should take my meds," I said.

"No, you most definitely should not do that," Loftus said. "You need to stop taking that crap and accept what you are."

"Thanks for the advice," I said. "But I don't think I'll be taking guidance from one of my hallucinations."

"Try something," Loftus said.

"Try something?" I cocked one eyebrow up at him.

"Yeah, like magic or a spell or something. Do some magic. That will prove you're a witch and I'm real," Loftus said.

"No, it won't," I countered. "It will just prove I'm even more delusional than Dr. Peterson thought."

"Do something that can't be explained away," Loftus said.

"Fine," I said and let out a deep sigh. I closed my eyes and concentrated as hard as I could before snapping my fingers. "There."

"What did you do?" Loftus asked.

"I turned on the shower," I said.

"No, you didn't," Loftus said as we both strained to hear if the shower was on.

It wasn't.

"My point exactly," I said. "But don't worry. I'm not going to take the meds. I've been taking them, and I can still see you. Obviously, they don't work."

"Hang on," Loftus said and he ran off toward the bathroom. "Hey, come in here," he called out after a few seconds.

I halfway expected Loftus to have disappeared when I walked into the bathroom, but he was still there sitting on the edge of the tub. When I looked at what he was pointing to, I saw that the showerhead was dripping pretty steadily.

"See," he said.

"That doesn't prove anything," I countered.

"Was it leaking yesterday?" Loftus asked. "Has it leaked like that the entire time you've been here?"

"No," I said.

It didn't prove anything, but it did give me pause. Loftus was right. The shower hadn't leaked at all since I'd moved into the room. Not even after I took a shower. It would turn completely off and stay off, but it was an old house.

"Do you see now?" Loftus asked. "Your powers aren't very strong, but that's because you just got them. We can work on that."

"I don't know…" I said but finding the shower dripping had caused something to click in my head.

"I've never met a necromancer before," Loftus said as he hopped down and started out of the bathroom.

"I am not a necromancer," I countered.

"You talk to the dead," he said plainly. "I know that because I've seen you talking to them. It's your strongest natural power."

"Maybe I'm just a medium then," I said. "Why do you immediately go to necromancer?"

"Mediums aren't witches, Hazel. They are mediums. You are a witch now, and your strongest power is talking to the dead. Look at your entire life. It's part of who you are," Loftus said.

"I wasn't born a witch, though," I said.

"Weren't you, though?" Loftus asked.

"No, I wasn't. That witch passed her powers onto me when she died," I said.

"But maybe you were born to get them," he said. "I doubt it was all a coincidence. Nothing ever is."

"If you say so," I said.

"Follow me," Loftus said and headed for the bedroom door.

"Where are we going?" I asked.

"Out to the garden to gather ingredients," he responded.

"To the poisoner's garden?" I couldn't believe it. I was not going to kill people.

"It's only poison if you do it wrong," he said with a chuckle. "The poison is in the dose."

"What about Rook?" I asked even as I opened the door and we walked out into the hallway.

"He's so absorbed in that program he's making, he'll never even notice we're out there," Loftus said.

"I don't know what to get," I said.

"That's where I come in," Loftus said. "I'm Loftus with the Mostus, and I'm your personal familiar."

Chapter Twelve

We spent a half an hour outside collecting leaves, berries, and flowers. After that, I went to the kitchen and fixed myself some French fries and chicken nuggets. Loftus had a small plate of cheese and crackers with two French fries on the side. He liked the fries a lot but said that he needed to watch his figure.

When I was done eating, I took a plate of fries and nuggets up to Rook's room. He was busy, as Loftus had said, but he took the food and a bottle of Coke with an appreciative smile. "Thank you," he said before closing the door. "I'll see you tomorrow. Glad you're feeling better," he called through the door.

"I am," I said as I walked down the stairs.

Loftus was trailing behind me. He'd hidden on the other side of the door while I delivered Rook's food, but he was back out in plain sight again.

"You're what?" he asked.

"I'm feeling better. I just realized that ever since I did the thing with the shower, I've been feeling much better," I said.

"Healing magic with necromancy?" Loftus said. "Interesting. Two sides of the same coin, but it's so rare for someone to have both."

"Thank goodness," I said.

"What?"

"That I have something other than death powers," I replied.

"So, you believe now?" he asked.

"I'm not willing to go that far yet, but I can't deny how I feel. Either you're right or I've had a complete psychotic break. I don't really care right now which it is. I'm just glad I don't feel like total crap anymore. I'm going to embrace it."

I'd started to feel better after the shower thing, but being out in the moonlight picking herbs and plants had practically supercharged me. It was so good that when we went back to my bedroom, I threw the heavy drapes open to let the moonlight into the room.

"When in Rome," I said to Loftus when he gave me a look.

I woke up the next morning to find Loftus asleep on the foot of my bed. In fact, he was snuggled up against my foot fast asleep.

A sudden, loud knocking at my bedroom door made us both jump halfway off the bed. "Hazel! It's Rook!"

"Who else would it be?" I called back as I slid off the bed and padded across the room.

"We have a funeral today. I can't believe I forgot," Rook said as I opened the door.

"What? How..."

"I don't know. Charlie scheduled it. It's on his calendar and not mine. With all the upheaval lately, I don't know. There's no excuse," Rook said.

"We haven't had a body come in," I said. "How?"

"He's down in the long-term storage. A member of his family couldn't get here for the funeral until today, so they've kept him on ice. I've got to get down there and get him ready for the service. The florist is going to be here soon," Rook was completely freaking out.

"It's going to be okay," I said. "We can do this together. I'll go let the florist in, and you go get the body ready. How long do we have?"

"The service isn't until ten," Rook said.

"We have like three hours then, right? Can you get the deceased ready for viewing by then?" I asked.

"He's already embalmed. I've just got to get him moved to the casket and do some final touch-up things," Rook said.

"See, we've got this," I said.

"I hope so," Rook said. "I've never messed up like this before. I've just been so distracted."

He pushed his glasses up on his nose and then turned and took off. Was he talking about me?

I mean, I could see how the disruption in his life could throw him off, but was I being more of a burden that I should? If nothing else, I could fix us some food.

I decided to make ham and cheese sandwiches. That way I could wrap one up and leave it in the fridge for Rook whenever he was ready. If I was going to be a source of distraction for him, then I would find ways to make up for it.

"So, the witch who gave me her powers, were you her familiar?"

Loftus sat on the kitchen floor on his butt with his little legs stuck out. He was gnawing on a piece of cheese I'd given him from the sandwiches. He held onto it with his front paws, and every time he took a bite, his wings shimmered. Loftus really liked cheese.

It was cliché, but it was also true.

"No, I wasn't. I've lived here for a very long time. I haven't been a familiar to any particular witch for centuries," Loftus said.

"Centuries?" I asked as I cut my sandwich in half. "Didn't you get bored and lonely?"

"That's how I ended up with these wings," he said.

"Do tell," I encouraged.

"I just got into it with a fae, and it cursed me. I was able to fend off most of the attack, but as you can see, not all of it," Loftus said.

"Fae?"

"Yes, the woods around Fullmourn are full of fae. Don't mess with them," he said and reached his arms out for more cheese.

"You mean like fairies?" I asked as I handed him another half slice of the sharp cheddar.

"Some of them are like that, but some of them not so much," he said. "They're all dangerous, though."

"So, in addition to witches and ghosts, you now want me to believe in fairies too?" I asked. "Anything else?"

"Vampires are definitely real," Loftus said. "It's a fae curse of the blood that can be passed on. So, definitely a thing."

"Werewolves?" I asked.

"Haven't met one," Loftus said.

"But they could be real?" I asked.

"Given everything I told you that is..." Loftus trailed off.

"I see your point," I returned. "Zombies?"

"Ah, we haven't had a good zombie outbreak in a century," Loftus said. "Maybe more. But yes, they exist. There are three kinds, though."

"Three kinds of zombies?" I asked before taking a bite of my sandwich.

"Again, there's a fae curse that can cause it. That's nasty stuff, but I don't even think it's the worst of what they are capable of. Second, there are the kind that your kind can raise. So, those are necromancy zombies. The third kind is demonic. I don't mess with demons. I don't know how they do it. Pretty sure it's some sort of incomplete possession of the dead or maybe them doing the opposite of healing. Everything they do is the opposite of the good power. But, like I said, I don't mess with demons, so I don't know," Loftus said.

"They are worse than fae?" I asked.

"There are some fae that are pretty dang close. In fact, I think they pal around from time to time. Man, that would be a bad day. Running into a demon and a fae hanging out," Loftus said. "Oh, and I think there are human causes for zombies too. You guys can't just leave well enough alone, and I think you've created a few viruses that can do the deed. If not, you've come mightily close."

"This is insane," I said. "I really am just hallucinating."

"Oh, boy," Loftus said. "I told you too much too soon. To be fair, you asked. If you didn't want to know the answer, maybe you shouldn't have asked."

"How was I supposed to know?" I said. "Like, the entire world, reality even, is completely different than what I believed."

"Take a deep breath," Loftus encouraged. "Think about it for a second. You humans are always making movies about this stuff. You love it. You can't get enough of it. Where do you think that comes from?"

"I don't know," I said, but he had a point. He hadn't told me anything existed that I'd never heard of before.

"It's because you all know. Deep down inside, every single human knows about and could see the real world around them if they wanted to see," Loftus said. "You guys are born with the ability to see and understand it all, and you teach yourselves to ignore it."

"Why would we do that?" I asked.

"Beats me, but I think it's something to do with a superiority complex. Anyway, all the witch did for you was unlock the door. She didn't really pass powers onto you. She passed her key. And before you say anything... not a literal key," Loftus said.

"I wasn't going to say that," I countered.

"Yes, you were. I could see it on your face," he said. "More cheese."

"What's the magic word?" I teased.

"Abracadabra," Loftus said and stuck his arms out to me.

The hair stuck up on the back of my neck, and a tingling sensation spread down my arms and my legs. My entire body buzzed with energy that seemed to come from everywhere outside of me and from the depths inside as well.

"Abrakadavra," I said, and the feeling stopped. Silence enveloped me as the chaos the first word created settled down. "What was that?"

"I didn't know that, like, you could actually use that word," he said with wide eyes. "It's just a silly saying for most people, but it had a real effect on you. I've never...and then you answered it... and..."

"I've heard that first word before," I said, but did not dare to speak the actual word again. "Magicians and stuff use it. Every cartoon about magic. Why would that have such an effect?"

"Because it's actually an ancient mystical spell, Hazel. It means, what I speak, I create. But, no one I've ever met can actually use it. Not really. But you should have seen you after I said it. You were practically glowing. That was nuts," Loftus said.

"The other word, the one I said after. I've never heard it before, but I answered with it. It made the buzzing stop," I said.

"It's the opposite of abra..." he cut himself off. "It's the opposite. It means, what I speak, I silence."

"Or destroy?" I asked.

"Yeah, that too," Loftus admitted. "I'm sorry. You've just got it in you. The power of light and dark. I know you don't like it, but it is what it is."

"There has to be something I can do," I said.

"To what? Destroy a part of yourself?" Loftus said. "No, you can't do that. Not without horrible consequences. But, you can do that thing with the wolves. You know, the thing?"

"The werewolves?" I asked.

"No, the story of the two wolves. They live inside of you or whatever. The one you feed is the one that gets strong. I don't know, lady. I've been trapped in a funeral home for hundreds of years."

"I know what you're talking about," I said. "So, I just have to feed the light, and everything will be fine."

"Sure," Loftus said before sticking his little paws out for more cheese.

After breakfast, I went out to the main entry area to wait for the florists. They arrived with three vans.

I propped the door open so that the florist and her assistant could bring everything in and set it up in the viewing room.

"Do you need any help?" I asked. "I wasn't expecting so many flowers."

"We don't usually have this many for one service, but don't worry. We have explicit instructions on where and how to place them. We'll get it done and get out of your hair," she said, and something flashed in her eyes.

If I was reading her correctly, it was a touch of fear and discomfort. She didn't like that part of her job. A lot of people didn't like dealing with death, so I understood. I wished I could help her, but I decided the best thing to do was just stay out of their way.

I didn't think it was very professional for me to just leave them unsupervised, though, so I grabbed the vacuum and started cleaning the entryway. When they were done unloading the flowers, I signed the invoice and moved on to vacuuming and dusting the viewing room.

When that was done, I debated between going to the basement to check on Rook or sweeping the front porch. I decided it was best to just stay out Rook's hair too and grabbed a broom to clean the outside front entrance and steps.

A while later, he emerged from the basement with the casket, and I helped him take it into the viewing room. We got it staged for the family, and Rook took a moment to survey the flowers.

"There's a sandwich in the fridge for you," I said. "I assume you didn't take time to eat this morning."

"Are you going to join me?" he asked.

"I already ate, so I'm going to go upstairs and get myself ready. I've got to wrangle my hair, makeup, and clothes," I said.

"Thanks for the sandwich," he said. "And for helping me pull this off. I can't believe we're ahead of schedule."

"I told you we could do this," I said.

After my shower, hair, and makeup, I found a folder slid under my bedroom door. In it were notes on conducting the service. It was some information on the deceased that Rook had collected from the family as well as notes on how to do things like welcome everyone to the service without sounding too cheery.

"Thanks," I said.

"For what?" Loftus appeared from his hole in the wall.

"Not you," I said. "I was thanking Rook for these notes."

"Rook's not here," Loftus said flatly.

I sighed and rolled my eyes. "It was symbolic."

"That's dumb. I will never understand you people," Loftus said.

"Did you need something?" I asked.

"How's it coming with George's murder?" Loftus asked.

"I don't know. Why don't you ask Nico? He's the sheriff," I said.

"Because George's ghost isn't standing in Nico's closet," Loftus said.

I whirled around, and sure enough, he was there. Just standing there in the open doorway of my closet staring at me with his teeth bared like a dog about to lunge.

"Loftus?" I wasn't sure if I was crying for help or asking what I should do.

"He seems to be getting pretty angry," Loftus said. "That happens when they are here for too long and have unresolved issues. Usually it takes longer than this, but it's not unheard of for someone of his character."

"George, I heard some things around town, and I found that scratch-off ticket. I gave it to Nico. You have to understand, though. I'm not the sheriff. I'm not even law enforcement. I have no authority to investigate your murder," I pleaded.

"And she doesn't like you," Loftus added.

I shot the mouse a look. "Loftus, dude, that's so not helpful."

George's ghost drifted out of the closet toward me. His eyes turned black, and he let out a low growling sound.

"I'll do what I can, I promise. I've got to work at this funeral, but after that, I promise you that I will figure this out. You have my word," I said. He kept coming toward me. "I know you're upset, but if you do anything to me, who will help you? No one else can see you or talk to you. You have to trust me."

He stopped. "One more day. I'll give you one more day," he snarled. "I'm starting to figure some things out, woman. I may not be able to sue you, but I can hurt you. I can hurt you and the people you care about."

And with that, he disappeared. The pressure in the room vanished too. I hadn't noticed the oppressive feeling in my bedroom until it was gone, but I needed to pay more attention. Perhaps that uncomfortable feeling in the air could help warn me when there was a nasty ghost nearby.

"How am I going to solve his murder in one day when the cops can't even solve it?" I asked Loftus.

He just shrugged and ran back into his hole.

"Thanks," I said, once again thanking someone who wasn't even there.

Chapter Thirteen

People started showing up for the funeral a half an hour early. I was glad that Rook and I had managed to get everything done ahead of time. The family was none the wiser that he'd forgotten their service.

He stuck around again to make sure I was okay. I felt better knowing he was in the back keeping an eye on things as I read the eulogy.

Well, as I read one paragraph of the eulogy. I was interrupted by the sound of rapid-fire sneezing and dramatic moaning.

It was the wife of the deceased. She was the reason the funeral has been postponed. Apparently, she'd been on some sort of spiritual retreat in Bali when her husband died and felt it was best if she "completed her journey" before she returned.

She'd forced the deceased's three children to postpone the funeral until she returned. Now, she sat in the front row sneezing and making this awful sound like a cat dying.

When the woman looked up at me, her eyes were bright red, and they were nearly as swollen as her lips. Ugly, angry red hives had broken out on her face and hands too.

"Oh, god, are those azaleas?" she cried out. "Oh, god, get me out of here!"

"Stepmother?" The deceased's daughter said menacingly. "Are you allergic to azaleas?"

"You know damn well I am, you ungrateful cow!" she cried out again and leapt out of her chair. "Get me out of here!"

No one moved to help her, though. Rook was out of his chair and moving up the aisle. I joined him, and we each took one of her arms.

"Come on, ma'am," Let's get you outside and get some air. "Hazel, call an ambulance. She might be going into anaphylactic shock."

"Is she going to die?" one of the deceased's sons asked casually. "That would be a real shame."

"Cody, hush," the daughter said. "I'll call the ambulance."

As it would turn out, the children were the ones who worked with the florist. For some reason, the flowers were arranged in such a way so that the azaleas were hidden. The stepmother hadn't seen them when she walked into the service.

Nico was out on the front porch of the funeral home, he'd arrived right after the ambulance, trying to figure out if he could or should arrest any of the deceased's grown children.

They were down at one end huddled together and whispering, and Nico and I were standing at other. "What do you think?" he asked me after taking some notes.

"About what?" I asked.

"About whether I should arrest one of them or all of them," he said.

"Why does everybody think I'm a cop?" I mused.

"What?" Nico looked at me like I had three heads.

"Nothing. I'm just being weird," I said. He looked at me like he didn't believe me. "My former boss asked me a lot of stuff that he should have known." It was true.

"So, you're saying I don't know how to do my job?" Nico asked.

"No," I said too quickly. "Not at all. I understand this is a weird circumstance. Probably not something you've had to deal with before."

"That's not why I'm asking you," he said and rubbed his stubbly, angular jaw. "I'm asking because you were inside with them when the incident happened. Did they say or do anything that made it obvious they tried to harm the woman?"

"Oh," I said and felt stupid. So, so stupid.

"So, did you?" Nico asked. "See or hear anything?"

"Nothing definitive," I said. "They obviously don't like her, but I wouldn't be comfortable saying they were trying to kill her or anything."

"That's what I thought," Nico said. "Well, the stepmother is at the hospital demanding to file a report, so I'm going to go talk to her."

"I'm sorry that I offended you," I said. "I can be a real jerk when I'm not thinking."

"I'm not offended," Nico said. "It takes a lot more than that."

194

"Good to know," I said. "Well, if you're not going to arrest them, then I am going to invite the deceased's children back inside to finish the services."

"Thank you!" the daughter said.

The man's children had been listening, and they all looked relieved. "Why don't we go back inside and let the sheriff deal with your stepmother," I said.

"I need to talk to you about something," Nico said as the three filed back into the funeral home. "Now isn't the time, but I'll need to call on you soon."

"You know where to find me," I said. "And you know how to get ahold of me."

"That I do," he said and tipped his hat to me.

I stood there for a moment and watched him walk to his cruiser. Rook stepped outside and joined me on the porch.

"He looks at you in a way that makes me uncomfortable," Rook said.

"The sheriff?" I asked. "Surely you don't think he's a threat?"

"Nothing like that," Rook said, and he turned to go back inside. "We should get the services going again. There are quite a few people inside who have been waiting too long to tell their loved one goodbye."

"I agree," I said.

What Rook said about the way Nico looked at me had me perplexed. I could tell he wasn't going to elaborate, though, and there was no point in trying to bug him about it.

"I want a cupcake," I said as Rook and I sat at the kitchen table after the funeral.

"Your appetite is returning," he said.

"I stopped taking the medication," I said. "I feel better."

"Do you feel better-better?" Rook asked.

"You mean, am I hallucinating?" I answered his question with a question.

"That is what I mean," he confirmed.

"I am not hallucinating," I said.

Technically, if Loftus the talking fairy mouse was to be believed, I wasn't hallucinating. So, it wasn't an outright lie. I couldn't tell Rook the details, but I sort of wished I could. I hadn't lived with anyone since college, and it had never been an easy experience for me, but living with Rook was different. I was comfortable having him around, and I wondered if he felt the same way.

"Even without the medicine?" he pressed.

"I think I was super sleep-deprived," I said. "I wasn't exactly sleeping well before I came to Fullmourn, and I believe the changes just pushed me over the edge. Sleep deprivation can have disastrous effects. If nothing else, the medicine made sure I got plenty of sleep."

"Well, if you have that much trouble sleeping again, take up running or try some Benadryl. You don't need antipsychotics for that," Rook said.

"Yes, sir," I said, and mock saluted him. "But, what about the cupcake? I feel like we need to focus here."

"The bakery is closed, but Mugs Coffee Shop sells her pastries. They might still have some cupcakes from today," Rook said. "I have a lot of work to do on my project, though."

"Fine, then I'll go by myself," I said and stood up.

"No, I'll go with you," he said and stood up too. "I haven't had a cupcake in a long time, and it might do me good to get out of the house every once in a while for something other than a funeral."

"Oooh, next thing you know, you'll be going to the grocery store with me," I teased.

"Don't push it," he said, but I could tell Rook was trying not to smile.

The coffee shop was quiet and practically abandoned. There was still a half an hour until they closed, so we were welcomed inside and encouraged to take a seat.

"You can sit," Rook said. "I'll grab the cupcakes and coffee? Do you want coffee this late?"

"I always want coffee," I said. "Two creams and four Splendas."

"Okay, I didn't sign up for all that," Rook said.

"Wait, are you teasing me?" I asked with mock indignation.

"No, I really mean you can get your own cream and sugar," Rook said completely deadpan.

"Oh," I said.

At that point, Rook cracked a real smile, but he quickly covered it with his hand and turned away. "Of course I'm joking. I'll be back in a minute."

I chose a table by the front window. As Rook walked up to the counter, a slender redhead with a perky smile and an even perkier...bust appeared from the back.

When she saw Rook, the wattage of her smile shot up to a million. I also watched as she sucked in her gut and pointed her high beams at him.

For some reason, it annoyed me, but what was even stranger was that Rook seemed to not even notice. He ordered the cupcakes and coffee, and then turned away from the counter while she filled the order.

He gave me a small wave when he caught me watching, and then pushed off the counter. "Could you bring it to our table?" he shot over his shoulder at the woman before proceeding over to me.

"She was working really hard for your attention," I said as he sat down.

"What?" he asked and then turned his head toward the counter. "You mean Agatha?"

"If that's her name," I said and realized my voice was dripping with...annoyance? Contempt? Whatever it was, I brushed it aside along with a crumb on the table that I swept onto the floor.

"The girl at the counter is Agatha," Rook confirmed. "What do you mean about her working hard for my attention?"

"I think she likes you," I said. "At the very least, she wanted you to notice her."

"It's hard not to notice her," he said, but there wasn't any appreciation in his voice. Rook sounded nearly as annoyed about the issue as I inexplicably felt.

"She's beautiful," I said. Why I felt the need to push it, I'd never know. "Maybe you should ask her out."

"Not interested," he practically grunted.

"Are you seeing someone else?" I asked as it occurred to me that we'd never discussed it. No woman had ever called on him at the funeral home, but I hadn't been there that long.

That question earned me a chuckle. "The kind of women who are attracted to a guy like me are only into it because of some strange fetish. One that I do not share. Makes a relationship, even of the casual sort, difficult."

"A guy like you?" I asked.

"Look at me," he said sharply, and I could have sworn a hint of red burned his cheeks.

But I had looked at him. Many times. He was tall and on the thin side, but not so much that he looked unhealthy... or unattractive even. His eyes were dark and intense, but there were plenty of woman that liked that sort of thing. He wore glasses, but they worked for him. His hair was thick and dark, but it was also shiny and soft. Well, I'd assumed it was soft. I hadn't actually ever touched his hair.

I found myself running my thumb over my fingertips as I imagined doing so. "I don't know what you mean," I said and flattened my hand on the table. My cheeks burned at the thought that Rook might somehow know I was imagining touching his hair.

"Are you all right?" he asked and pressed his lips into a line.

Before I could answer, Agatha bounced up to the table and slid the tray in front of Rook. She thrust her ample bosom into his face. "The cupcakes are my special recipe," she said.

I bet they are, Agatha, I thought.

"They're letting you bake now?" Rook asked.

She giggled and set a plate and coffee mug in front of him. When she took mine off the tray, Agatha left them in the middle of the table. She was trying hard to pretend I wasn't there.

"Have you met my cousin, Hazel?" Rook asked.

"Oh, you're his cousin? That's so nice," she said and looked at me like I was his annoying little cousin he'd had to drag along.

"We're not really related," I snarked and kicked him under the table. I don't know why I did it, but I totally did. "We are living together, though."

"What?" Agatha nearly dropped the tray at that.

"Yeah," I said. "I've moved into the funeral home. You may have heard that I inherited it. I'm Rook's boss now too. He has to do whatever I tell him."

Agatha looked horrified, and I was living for every single second of it. "Oh," she said.

"Say, Agatha, could you bring us some cream and Splenda?" Rook asked as I swore Agatha's bottom lip began to quiver.

"Yes," she said. "I can do that for you, Rook."

"It's for me," I said.

All the wind went out of her again, and Agatha huffed as she practically stomped off back to the counter.

"Why did you do that?" Rook asked with one eyebrow cocked up.

"I don't know," I said and bit my bottom lip. "She kinda annoys me," I leaned over and whispered. "I'm sorry."

"Don't be sorry," he said and laughed. "I'm glad I let you talk me into coming with you. I'm enjoying your petty side."

"I am being petty, aren't I?" I asked. "I will try to do better."

Agatha brought our cream and Splenda over to the table. She didn't get to stay and vie for Rook's attention any longer, though. A pair of older women came into the shop in a rush.

"Do we have time for a coffee?" one of them, wearing a purple turtleneck and pressed khakis, asked.

"Oh, and a couple of those cinnamon rolls," the other one, in black leggings and a floral hi-lo top, added. She put one hand on her stomach and fluffed her chin-length bob with the other. "I'm starving."

"Sure thing," Agatha said with a bright smile.

She went back up to the counter and began preparing their order. When I looked back at Rook, he was playing chess on his phone.

"You winning?" I asked.

"Unfortunately, no," he said and put his phone face down on the table.

"You don't have to stop on account of me," I said.

"I don't," he said, "but I'd rather spend this time with you."

"We live together," I said. "Well, I mean we live in the same house. We don't live together despite what I told Agatha."

"So?" Rook asked.

"So, we're together all of the time," I said. "You're not sick of me yet?"

"Why would I be?" Rook said. "Besides, we're not together all of the time. I'm always locking myself away in my room to work on my project. I'm sorry about that."

"You don't have to be sorry," I said. "It's important to you, and it's not like I'm your responsibility. I mean, entertaining me and all that."

"That's probably good for you," he said with a chuckle.

"There you go again hinting that you're not an amazing dude," I said and then stuffed half the cupcake into my mouth.

"Did you really just call me an amazing dude?" he asked.

I shook my head no because my mouth was still full. Rook just shrugged his shoulders and began eating his cupcake.

As I was trying to wash some of the cake down with coffee, the two women who had come in sat down at a table a few feet from us.

"Is that her?" Purple Turtleneck asked. She was obviously unaware that her voice could travel seven feet.

"I think so. She's with him, so it must be," Black Leggings confirmed.

"Did you hear they're saying she did it?" Turtleneck whisper-yelled.

"No way," Leggings answered.

"You're right, there is no way," Turtleneck said as she looked me over.

Rook looked like he was about to say something, but I put my hand up for him to stop. They were talking about George Cadell. I just knew it, and I wanted to hear what they had to say.

"Who do you think it was?" Leggings asked.

Yes, purple turtleneck lady, who do you think it was? I thought. I even leaned in and didn't care that Rook was judging me.

"Well, you know he owed Rocky a ton of money," Turtleneck said.

"Rocky Heimer?" Leggings asked.

"Yeah," Turtleneck confirmed.

"Why did he owe him money? How did someone like George end up mixed up with someone like Rocky?" Leggings asked.

"I have no idea," Turtleneck said. "I don't run around in those kinds of circles."

"Where did you hear it, then?" Leggings asked.

"Everybody knows," Turtleneck said haughtily.

Obviously, everybody didn't because she didn't even know what George owed the money for, but it still made me wonder. Was he in bad debt with someone? Was that why he was so obsessed with scratch-off tickets?

"Who is Rocky Heimer?" I asked Rook as we got back into his car.

"He fancies himself as somewhat of a local mobster," Rook said. "I don't know if he's actually in the mob or not, but he's involved in drugs, girls, and some petty crime stuff. That I know of. Why?"

"I just heard those women talking about George's death," I said. "I'm curious."

"Why are you still worried about that?" Rook asked obliviously.

He didn't know that George's ghost was threatening me, and I wasn't about to tell him. He'd drive me to the state hospital right then and there. All that stuff about not needing drugs would be right out the window.

"Because I'm still technically a suspect," I said, and it was true.

"They're never going to arrest you for George's murder," Rook said. "You should put that out of your head. You've got enough to worry about."

I couldn't just let it go, though. George Cadell sat in the back seat of Rook's car staring at me in the rearview mirror.

I was running out of time.

Chapter Fourteen

Once Rook was upstairs deep into working on his project, I slipped out the side door and into my car. My destination was George Cadell's house. A quick internet search was all it took to find his address, and I was on my way.

Halfway there, my purse began to thrash around. I'd placed it on the passenger seat when I got into the car, and it took all of my focus to keep my eyes on the road and not the wriggling mass inside of my bag.

For a moment, it was terrifying. I started to pull the car over to the curb when Loftus's little head popped out the top.

"You scared the crap out of me," I said as I checked for cars and pulled back out onto the road.

"What did you think was in your purse?" he asked. "Like, I'm genuinely curious what you thought could be in your purse that was scary."

"I..." I started to say.

"Wait. I was just in there. I know how scary it is," he snarked.

"Nobody asked you to hide in my purse and stow away on my mission," I said.

"Okay," Loftus began, "I don't know if you've just never seen a witch movie or television show or what, but do you really not know how the familiar thing works?"

"You don't have to be a butthead about it," I said.

"Oh, but I do," Loftus retorted. "I so totally do."

"So, you're here to help me and protect me?" I asked.

"Yes," Loftus responded.

"And you're going to come with me wherever I go whether I want you to or not?" I asked.

"Look, it's the job. I'm on your side, so it's not like I'm going to turn you into the cops or anything," Loftus said as he settled on top of my purse and made himself comfortable.

"What would you tell the cops?" I asked a little too defensively.

"Where are we going?" He answered my question with a question. Not fair.

"Well, we're going over to George Cadell's house to see if there is anything we can find about his death," I said.

"And how are we going to do that?" Loftus asked. "Are we going to be able to investigate from the sidewalk?"

"We're going to have to let ourselves in," I admitted. "Look, I don't want to do this. I know we shouldn't be breaking into a dead man's house and going through his things, but we have to figure this out. I have to figure this out. I cannot let people I love get hurt."

Loftus seemed to think it over for a second. "I'll do my best to protect you and keep you from getting caught."

"Thank you," I said.

The fact that I was thanking a talking mouse with fairy wings for vowing to protect me while I broke into a man's house, to solve his murder because a ghost was going to start hurting the people I loved, was not lost on me. Either I had accepted who I was, or I had completely lost my mind.

Maybe both. Probably both.

I parked a couple of blocks away from George's address in an alley. The last thing I needed was for a neighbor to call the sheriff while I had my car parked out front so I couldn't escape.

We were walking down the street, trying to look inconspicuous, when George's next-door neighbor came outside. He was dressed in white and blue striped pajama pants and a navy t-shirt. Over the top of that he had an old gray bathrobe, and he was watching us.

"Hello," I said and waved at him. The man looked startled that I acknowledged him, so I kept pretending like he was the person I was looking for instead of getting ready to break into his dead neighbor's house.

"Hello," he finally managed back. "Can I help you with something?"

"You sure can," I said enthusiastically. "You are just the person I was hoping to speak with."

"I am?" he asked.

"You're George Cadell's next-door neighbor, right?" I asked.

"That I am," he admitted. "What's this about?"

I made my way up his sidewalk and stood at the base of his front steps. "I wanted to ask you about George," I said. "I know it's strange, but there are some things that are bothering me."

"You're that new funeral director, right?" he asked.

"I am," I said.

"You working with the sheriff or something? I thought that was the medical examiner's job. Or maybe the coroner, but we don't have one of those," he said.

"I'm not," I said. "It's more for my own peace of mind. I understand if you don't want to talk to me. You don't have to if you're not comfortable."

He took the bait. "It's fine," he said. "Having a conversation with a lovely young woman isn't something that's going to make a grizzled old fellow like me uncomfortable."

"I didn't think so," I said. "Why I'm here is because I've heard some things around town about George and his behavior. People have said some concerning things, and I figured you'd know as well as anyone."

"Well, I've heard that you possibly had a run-in with the old goat yourself," the man said with a chuckle. "We should make our formal introductions before you go accusing me of murder, though. My name's Mike."

"I'm Hazel," I said, "but you already knew that, right?"

"That I did," he said and tightened the belt on his bathrobe.

"It's nice to meet you, Mike," I said. "And I'm not here to accuse you of murder."

"It's nice to meet you too, Hazel. Glad I got the chance while I am still on this side of the grass. So, tell me, Hazel the funeral director, what particular aspect of George's behavior can I help you with?" Mike asked.

"I'll just come out and say it. I heard the two of you got into it, and he poisoned your lawn. Did he do things like that a lot of people? Does anyone who took it particularly hard stick out to you?" I asked.

"So, you are here to accuse me of murder," Mike said with another chuckle.

"I'm not," I said. "I'm really not trying to insinuate that you killed a man over grass. I just want to know if there is anyone else that George hurt? Maybe he did worse to someone else, or maybe they didn't take it as well as you did."

"Well, first I should clear the air about the grass," Mike said. "I thought he did it. We even got into a screaming row in our front yards over it. In a moment of anger, I may have threatened to beat him to death with my rake. But he didn't do it."

"What?" I asked.

"After I got so heated about the whole thing, George sent some lawncare guy over here to look at my lawn. The guy took a bunch of tests and it turned out I had some weird fungus thing in my soil. George did not poison my grass, and after a couple of treatments, my lawn was as good as new," Mike said. "I apologized to George."

"Oh," I said.

"Yeah, and after that, I guess you could have called us friends. Maybe not best buddies or anything, but we'd have a beer together some nights. He taught me how to play chess," Mike said.

"I'm sorry for your loss, then," I said.

"No mind," Mike said. "George wouldn't want me getting all weepy and pathetic over him."

"So, then you don't think he did something to someone that would make them actually want to beat him to death with a rake?" I asked.

"George could be a crotchety old fool, and I think that gave people the wrong idea about him. Didn't matter that his bark was worse than his bite. He gave people's imaginations plenty of ammunition. In a town like this, that's all it takes."

After that, Mike invited me to sit on his porch and have a beer, but I declined. Actually, I offered a rain check on the idea. He seemed nice and kinda lonely, so I figured it wouldn't hurt to come back some time and hang out.

I had to pretend that I was going back the way I came until Mike went back into his house and shut off his porch light. Once he did, I watched from behind a bush, I went back around the block the other way and approached George's house from the other side.

George's neighbor on the other side had all of their lights out. Either they were already in bed or were not home. So, I was able to make it up George's driveway, around to his back yard, and finally up to his back door without any other neighbors popping out for a chat.

Police tape had hung across the back door, but it had either been cut or had come off on its own. It dangled from the doorframe, no longer blocking passage into the house.

It occurred to me, as I was reaching out for the doorknob, that the house was probably locked up. I tried the knob, and sure enough, it didn't turn.

I'd seen people pick locks in movies. How hard could it be? I just had to do something with the tumblers and jiggling. Time was of the essence, though, so I reached into my purse and pulled out a couple of bobby pins.

After getting down on my knees so the knob was eye level, and setting my purse next to my leg, I went to work jamming the bobby pins into the lock and wiggling.

"What are you doing?" Loftus's head popped out of my purse.

"Shhh," I whispered to him. "Someone's going to hear me."

"No one can hear me but you and possibly other witches. They can hear you," he said.

"Then stop talking to me," I hissed. "I'm picking the lock."

"Do you know how to pick a lock?" he asked.

I shook my head no, but I persisted undeterred. Eventually, I heard a couple of subtle clicks, and the door popped open. Thankfully, the deadbolt hadn't been engaged, and my leaning on the door caused the little doohickey to clear the strike plate.

"Ha!" I said and stood up.

"That was lucky," Loftus said as he ducked back down into my purse.

I picked it up, hung it over my shoulder, and proceeded inside George's kitchen. Someone had left the light over the sink on, so there was enough illumination that I didn't need to use a flashlight. Turning on another light was out of the question too. Someone would definitely see that.

My next step after closing the door and locking it behind me was to figure out what to do next. I was woefully unprepared in the breaking and entering department. I hadn't planned any of it out, and I didn't know what I was looking for now that I was inside.

"Put me down," Loftus said from inside my purse.

I set my purse down for a moment and let him climb out. He immediately ran out of the kitchen.

"Loftus!" I called after him.

"Keep it down," he said. "The neighbors will hear you hollering like that. I'm doing some recon, so stay put."

Not knowing any better course of action, I stood in the kitchen waiting for Loftus to do his thing. He eventually came back and stood in the doorway.

"The curtains are all open, so between the moonlight and the streetlights, you'll be able to see. But, you're going to have to crawl. You've got to stay under the windows," he said.

The one-story house had a kitchen that led out into a large room that functioned as both the dining room and the living room. On the other side of the living room was a short hallway. At each end of the hallway was a bedroom, and right smack dab in the middle off the living room was the house's only bathroom.

There was nothing on any of the counters or the tables. In fact, George didn't seem to own much. He didn't have any photos on the walls or knick-knacks. That wasn't too hard to believe given that he was a man, but it was difficult to wrap my head around the fact that no girlfriend, wife, or even his mother, had ever given him any kind of keepsake. Perhaps they had and he'd either thrown them away or kept them stored out of sight.

I learned all of this on my hands and knees fumbling around in the dark. It made it rather hard to actually search for anything... until I got to the bedroom.

What I found was a box. It was an old cardboard shoebox pushed under the bed. There were a few things inside, but the two items that got my attention were a scrap of paper with Rocky's address on it and a photograph of a young woman.

The woman in the photo looked like she could be George's daughter or perhaps granddaughter depending on how recently someone snapped the picture.

She also seemed to be completely unaware that she was being watched or photographed. The snapshot had been taken from across the road while she unloaded grocery bags from a car.

Was it a threat? Had someone, perhaps this Rocky person, used someone George loved as leverage to get payment? It all fit together given what I'd learned in the coffee shop, but was it real?

Or was I making connections that didn't exist? Basically, I'd concocted an entire story in my head.

"I don't know," I said to Loftus. He'd come into the room and plopped down next to the box.

"What don't you know?" he asked.

I explained what I'd learned at the coffee house and my theory. Without really thinking about it, I tucked the address into my purse.

Maybe it was nothing if the deputies who searched the house had left it behind. Or perhaps they already had Rocky's address and the little slip of paper wasn't actual evidence.

One thing was abundantly clear. I had no idea what I was doing. What was also obvious was that if I was going to solve George's murder, I was probably going to have to do something stupid.

My next move was to go see about Rocky.

Chapter Fifteen

When I pushed the box back under the bed and then got back up on my knees, George was there sitting on the edge of the bed. The sight of him took my breath away, but he wasn't snarling at me.

"I'm going to go see Rocky," I said.

George's ghost nodded at me.

"Do you think he killed you?" I asked. "Or maybe had you killed?"

He just shrugged at me.

So helpful...

"The girl in the picture, is she related to you?"

He nodded yes.

"Is she your daughter?"

He nodded no.

"Your granddaughter?"

He nodded yes.

So, the picture was recent. "Was Rocky using her to threaten you? Why aren't you talking now?"

George's spirit looked sad, but he wasn't really looking at me anymore. His ghost was much more transparent than he'd been when he appeared to me earlier. I reasoned that he had less power. Some of the anger and fight had gone out of him, and that seemed to make his tether to the world weaker.

How I knew that, I had no idea, but I felt it. I could feel that he was drifting away.

"He'll come back," Loftus said when George's ghost flickered out. "I know what you're thinking, but he'll come back."

"You don't think that maybe he's accepted his fate now? Perhaps I could stop doing this," I said.

"He's probably just charging up again," Loftus said. "Maybe he came back too soon this time. We should keep going."

"All right, let's go talk to Rocky," I said.

I crawled back through the house and then went out the back door. I'd put Loftus back in my purse at that point, but I briefly considered having him recon the driveway and the street to see if any neighbors were out.

My question was answered when red and blue lights lit up the driveway. Someone had called the sheriff.

I could not get caught breaking and entering into George Cadell's house. Leaving the way we came was out, so I had to make a break for it across the back yard.

Figuring that I had seconds before Nico or one of his deputies appeared in the back yard, I clutched my purse to my chest and ran. "You're squishing meeeeeee!!!" Loftus cried out from inside the bag.

It was lucky no one else could hear him because it was one heck of a wail. I moved my arm and felt him shifting around inside the bag. But I kept running.

The back yard was surrounded by an old chain-link fence, and there was a gate that opened up into an overgrown alley. It seemed as though my luck had run out because there was a chain around the gate and post. It was padlocked shut.

There was no time to think or panic. I dropped my purse as gently as I could on the other side of the fence and began to climb over it.

Loftus peeked out just in time to see my toe catch on the top of the fence. I fell face-first into the weeds. Underneath the itchy plants was a gravel alley that cut my palms and face.

There was no time to worry about a few scrapes. I snatched my purse off the ground and ran down the alley with all of my might.

I wasn't much of a sprinter, but adrenaline coursed through my veins. When I got to the end of the alley, I looked both ways. There were no cops and no neighbors around.

So, I turned the corner out of the alley, hooked my purse over my shoulder, and casually walked the rest of the way to my car. It took every ounce of strength and discipline I had to maintain a slow, measured pace. Everything in me wanted to run the rest of the way to the car and get the heck out of there. But I had to be cool. I had to pretend I wasn't up to anything suspicious or someone might notice me.

After I was behind the wheel of my car, doors locked, and Loftus sitting on the passenger seat staring at me, I noticed that I'd ripped the knees on my jeans. "That's the style now," Loftus said when he saw me playing with the frayed fabric.

"Are the skinned knees underneath fashionable too?" I asked.

"Very chic," Loftus said. "Classy even."

I rolled my eyes and got ready to put my key in the ignition when my phone rang. I took it out of my purse and checked the number. It looked familiar, but I couldn't quite put my finger on it at first.

After a second of wracking my brain, I realized it was Dr. Peterson. I hit the button to silence the ringer, and thanked the stars that he hadn't called while I was fleeing from the police, before putting the phone back down on the seat.

Next to Loftus...

The flying fairy mouse...

I'd just broken into a house and fled from the sheriff...

The phone started ringing again. I picked it up and it was Dr. Peterson again. Curiosity about why he'd called twice overrode my desire to not talk to him in the moment.

"Hello," I said when I picked up.

"Hazel, I'm glad I caught you," he said cheerfully. "Sorry to call twice in a row, but sometimes people don't make it to the phone in time, and it's important that I check in with you."

"Check in with me?" I asked.

"About your new meds. How are they working out for you?" he asked.

I took a deep breath and looked over at Loftus the flying fairy mouse who was staring at me from the passenger seat again. "I stopped taking them," I admitted.

"What?" Dr. Peterson seemed rattled by my revelation, but when he continued, he sounded calmer and more professional. "Ms. Holloway, we need to discuss this."

"I can make an appointment for later in the week," I said. "We can discuss it, but those medicines made me feel terrible, Dr. Peterson. I cannot live my life like that."

"You should come in now," he said.

"It's nighttime," I said. "Your office closed almost four hours ago."

"I'll make an exception," he said. "You can't just stop taking those medicines. They can have horrible side effects if you don't wean yourself off them properly."

You mean like increased hallucinations and criminal behavior? I thought but did not say.

I looked at Loftus again. He was still staring at me with his sparkling wings fluttering gently behind him. Suddenly, I found myself unsure of things I'd been nearly certain of earlier in the day.

The possibility that I was having a total psychotic break, and it had led me to break the law, came crashing down on me. What was I thinking? What was I doing?

"I'll come in," I said. "I can be there in a few minutes."

"Great. Hey, pull all the way into the driveway up to the garage. I don't want anybody seeing your car and thinking that someone is breaking in. I'll leave the back door unlocked for you," Dr. Peterson said.

"Thank you. I'll see you soon," I said.

We disconnected and Loftus let out a loud huff. "You are not going to let him talk you into taking those horrible pills again, are you?" he asked.

I contemplated whether I should say anything or not. If Loftus was a hallucination, and at the time I thought he probably was, it wouldn't do my mental health any good to keep talking to him. It appeared that acknowledging the delusions only made them stronger.

"Hazel," Loftus said softly.

"I don't know," I said and started the car.

"You don't know what?" Loftus asked.

"I want you to be real. It would be heartbreaking if you weren't."

"I am real," Loftus said. "We've been over this. You shouldn't go see this doctor. I don't like it."

"That's the exact thing a hallucination who didn't want to be eliminated would say," I said.

"Eliminated? What?" Loftus sounded a bit nervous. "Wait, if I was just your imagination, why would I care? You couldn't really get rid of me. I'd just come back as something else. Hazel, please. The medicine that doctor gave you made you really sick. If you want to talk to a psychiatrist, fine, but find someone else."

That kind of stuck with me a little bit. If Loftus was just a hallucination trying to save his own behind, why would he encourage me to see a different doctor?

"He said it's dangerous for me to just stop taking the meds," I said. "I at least need to hear him out about that. I'm not saying that I'll start taking them again, but I don't want to get sicker."

"You're feeling fine, right?" Loftus asked.

Physically, I was. After I'd stopped taking those pills, a weight had lifted off of my body. I felt lighter, my nausea was gone, and I even found myself craving some chicken nuggets dipped in sweet chili sauce. I was definitely going to have that when I went home.

"I feel good," I said. "But you're still here. George is still around threatening me."

"Thanks," Loftus said and rolled his eyes.

"I don't mean it like that," I said.

"You do," Loftus said. "You're saying that something's wrong with you because I'm here. You'd be better off if I wasn't around."

"Loftus, cut it out," I said. "You're not going to guilt trip me. I'm just going to explain to Dr. Peterson that I'm fine, okay? Then we'll go home and have chicken nuggets. I promise."

"You could tell him that over an email," Loftus protested.

"Fine," I said and pulled the car over to the curb. "I'll call him and tell him I'm not coming. Will that make you happy?"

"Very," Loftus said.

"I'm not promising that I won't see someone else," I said.

"Understood," Loftus said.

I pulled out my phone and called Dr. Peterson's number. He picked up on the second ring.

"Hazel, are you here?" he asked. "I don't see your car."

"I think I'm just going to go home, Dr. Peterson. I really don't want to be on the medication anymore, and I'm feeling fine," I said.

He was silent for a few seconds. "It's entirely up to you, Hazel, but since I'm treating you for a major psychiatric disorder, there are a couple of forms I need you to sign."

"What? You said before that I didn't have a major psychiatric disorder," I said. I was growing agitated with the entire situation.

"Someone with your level of depression and anxiety is still suffering from major issues. If you don't want to see me for them, that's fine, but I need a patient release form. It's basically like you checking out of the hospital against medical advice. I am advising you not to discontinue care, but I can't stop you."

"And you need this form tonight?" I asked. "It couldn't wait until tomorrow?"

"You're not taking the medications I prescribed to you. If something were to happen to you because of your refusal to comply with your medical regimen, I don't want to take a chance of being liable. Please just come sign the form. It will only take you a few minutes," Dr. Peterson sounded tired and exasperated.

It made me feel a bit guilty. "Okay," I said. "I'll come sign the form. After all, you're not liable. This is my decision."

"Very good. I will see you soon," he said and hung up.

"You're still going over there?" Loftus asked.

"He's just got some form for me to sign. We'll be in and out," I said. "And then that's the end of it."

"I still don't see why you can't do it over email," Loftus protested.

"It's a medical form. I guess he needs a real signature," I said. "We're getting it over with, okay?"

"Fine," Loftus said.

I pulled back out onto the street and drove the rest of the way to Dr. Peterson's office. After pulling all the way into the driveway like he asked, I shut the car off and looked at the house.

There were lights on in the upstairs windows, and it dawned on me that he was probably living above his office. No wonder he didn't think it was a big deal to do the paperwork at such a strange hour.

"You coming in or staying out here?" I asked Loftus.

He answered by wiggling his way into my purse. I felt a little better having Loftus with me. I had no idea why, but with him in my purse, I felt more secure.

The back door was open, so I went inside. No one was in the room, which had been a kitchen at one point but had been converted into what looked like a break room. There was still a fridge and microwave, but most of the counters and other appliances were missing. There was also a large table with six chairs. On top of it were a used coffee cup and a few magazines.

I walked through the house until I found my way back to the entry area. From there I managed to get to Dr. Peterson's office.

That door was open as well, but when I walked inside, he wasn't there. My dilemma was that I wasn't sure if I should wait for him in his office or go back out into the entry area.

"Dr. Peterson," I called out. "Sorry, I thought you'd be in here."

"I'll be down in a moment," he yelled from what I assumed was upstairs. He'd sounded quiet and far away.

Since I wasn't there for an actual appointment, I decided it would be better for me to wait out front. As I was leaving his office, something on his desk caught my eye.

It was a pile of scratch-off tickets. The same kind as the one I'd found under my front porch.

Suddenly, my vision narrowed, and I was in my mind's eye looking back at the memory of George Cadell in the gas station. He was scratching off his ticket at the counter, and it was not the same as the ones on Dr. Peterson's desk or the one I found under my porch.

George's ticket had been blue with trains on it. Dr. Peterson's were red with little food icons. Was it possible that the ticket I found under my front porch wasn't George's at all? Could it have been Dr. Peterson's?

But why?

I hadn't even realized I'd picked the pile of tickets up until Dr. Peterson walked into the office and saw me holding them. "What are you doing in here?"

I watched as his eyes went from me to the tickets in my hand. His brow furrowed and red burned from under his collar all the way up to his cheeks. Dr. Peterson looked like he was barely containing an insidious rage.

"I thought you were in here waiting for me," I said. "The back door was open."

"I left it unlocked for you, but I thought you'd wait in there or maybe in the reception area.

Why are you in my office going through my things?"

"They were sitting on your desk," I said as I gingerly put them back down.

"Why are you picking up things off my desk?" he asked and took a huge step toward me. "Did you go through anything else?"

"I didn't," I said. "I only picked them up because I found one like it the other day. Outside my house. It was there under the porch after they took George's body away."

The look in Dr. Peterson's eyes darkened, but a terrifying calm took over his face. "It's a shame that you wouldn't take your medicine, Hazel. I'm going to have to have you put in the hospital on a psych hold now. It's what's best for you and the community. You are a danger to yourself and others."

"What?" I asked.

"It will be easier and safer for you if you just comply," he said. "Unfortunately, others have not, and they've met terrible consequences."

"You're talking about George Cadell. You tried to put him in a mental hospital, didn't you?

And he fought back?" I asked. "You killed him? You have to realize I'm going to tell them."

I regretted saying that part because I'd basically invited him to kill me. It had just slipped out because I was panicking a bit.

A broad smile that didn't reach his eyes crossed Dr. Peterson's face. I saw for the first time how malevolent he really was. "No one will believe you. I'm a highly respected psychiatrist with an excellent history of patient care, and you're the new girl in town. The new girl with a history of hallucinations, I might add. Oh, and you stopped taking your medication and had a psychotic break. It's unfortunate, but the hospital is where you belong."

He took out his phone and started to dial a number when someone stepped into the office behind him. It was a pale, gaunt young man in what looked like hospital scrubs. Behind him, George Cadell's ghost materialized.

"Dr. Peterson," the young man's voice was gravely but sure. "I need to speak with you."

George's spirit studied me for a moment, and I think my look of panic and fear registered with him. I pointed at the pile of scratch-off tickets on the desk, and his eyes followed my gesture.

He stood there for a moment, and I saw the look of realization dawn on his face. He remembered.

That realization turned into fury, and before anyone could say anything else, George's ghost dove into the young man. The man blinked as George possessed him, and George shook his arms and cracked his neck. It was like he was getting himself used to the body he'd inhabited.

"You did this to me," George said and pointed at Dr. Peterson.

"Kyle, you needed to be in the hospital. You're a very sick young man," Dr. Peterson said. Obviously, he thought he was still speaking to Kyle and had no idea that George was using the guy to communicate. "How did you get out?"

"An angel helped me escape," George said sarcastically. He must have been referring to himself, but why had he helped the kid escape the mental hospital? He didn't know Dr. Peterson had done it, so that only left one possibility. He'd helped a mental patient escape to come after me because I hadn't solved his murder fast enough.

But, that was neither here nor there at the time.

"I guess I'm going to need two transports," Dr. Peterson said as he dialed the phone. "Kyle, you need to go back. The hospital is the safest place for you. Ms. Holloway, it's going to be the best place for you too."

"You can't just get rid of people by sticking them in a mental hospital," George said. "Eventually, people will catch on to what you're doing."

"I'm doing my job," Dr. Peterson said, and he really sounded like he believed that. "I'm saving people."

The level of narcissism it must have taken to believe that was stunning. Dr. Peterson seemed to have zero self-awareness. He was the one who was a danger to himself and others.

"You killed George Cadell because he wouldn't go down without a fight," I said. "And now you want to lock me away because I know. When will it end?"

"Hopefully, it will end with you," he said as he waited for someone on the other end to pick up.

"Why?" I asked. "Why did you kill George? Why did you want him in the hospital? He wasn't your patient, was he?"

George was the one who answered. "I was for a short time. He convinced me to come see him. Then he put me on a bunch of medications that made me really sick." This all sounded really familiar. "I wanted to stop taking them, but he started threatening me. Said I was too big of a liability."

"Why?" I turned to George.

"Because I saw him somewhere he didn't want to be seen," George said.

"Damnit, voicemail," Dr. Peterson said. He slammed his phone down on his desk. "I guess I'll just have to take you there myself."

"Where did you see him?" I asked George.

Dr. Peterson hadn't been paying attention to our conversation, but he turned his attention to us. "You both really are crazy."

"I saw him at a gambler's anonymous meeting," George said.

All the color drained out of Dr. Peterson's face. It was something he obviously didn't want anyone to know. A secret worth killing over.

"How do you know that?" he asked because he still thought he was talking to Kyle.

"Don't you recognize me, Doc?" George taunted.

Dr. Peterson cocked his head to the side like a puppy trying to hear something. He studied Kyle for a second, and then he saw. He saw something that told him he was really speaking to George. Maybe it was in the eyes, or perhaps he could see George's spirit manifesting. I don't know for sure, but whatever it was, he knew.

"How? How is that even possible?" He ran his hands roughly through his hair. "This isn't happening. You're gone. I made sure of it!"

"You made sure I was dead, but I'm not gone," George said.

Dr. Peterson lost it.

Without another word, he lunged for Kyle. I watched in horror as the doctor knocked Kyle's body to the floor and wrapped his hands around the young man's throat. The same way George had died.

But George was a much older man. Kyle was still young and strong, and George used the younger man's strength to throw Dr. Peterson off of him.

Loftus emerged from my purse with a piercing squeak. It caught Dr. Peterson off guard, and as Loftus ran around to bite the doctor's ankle, George grabbed a bust of Lincoln off one of the bookshelves in the office.

Dr. Peterson kicked Loftus and sent him sliding across the hardwood floor. I saw red. Fury at him hurting my familiar made my blood boil.

But I didn't get the chance to fight. Dr. Peterson came at me, but George lifted the bust statue high, and brought it down on Dr. Peterson's head with a loud thud.

The doctor crumpled to the floor. Kyle's strength meant that it only took one good whack, and Peterson was dead.

I saw the moment he died, and his spirit left his body. He tried, even after dying, to reach out and grab me. But it was him who got snatched up. The floor underneath him glowed red, and black hands reached up and wrapped around his feet and ankles. His spirit was dragged down into whatever lay beneath.

By the time Nico arrived, George's spirit had gone to the other side. Solving the crime really had released him to move on, and saving my life had redeemed him. If he even needed to be redeemed. Heck, I guessed we all probably did.

Kyle was very confused, but when I told him that he'd saved my life, he hugged me. When Kyle came to and saw Dr. Peterson, he thought for sure he'd go down for murder.

I'd find out later that, like many of Dr. Peterson's patients, Kyle didn't need to be institutionalized. Because he was cleared of Dr. Peterson's death, he was quickly released.

After answering all of Nico's questions, I got to go home too. "I need to talk to you," he said as I was leaving.

"I thought I answered all of your questions," I said.

"You did. This is about a more… personal matter, but it can wait," he said. "Can I call on you again soon?"

"Sure," I said. "Is everything all right?"

"It is," he confirmed. "I'll see you soon, Hazel."

I left quickly after that. I had Loftus tucked into my purse, but he hadn't woken up. I needed to get somewhere I could look him over. When I'd scooped him up off the floor to hide him, he was limp but still breathing.

We went home, and I snuck into the house and up to my room. I laid Loftus out on the bed and put my hands over him. While I had no idea what I was doing, I knew I had to try.

With my eyes closed tight, I imagined a white light. The image came to me rather than me conjuring it. Something was guiding me, but I didn't question it. The light was in my chest around my heart, and I used my energy to push it down my arms into my hands. When the light reached my hands, I drove it, as gently as I could, into Loftus.

He jumped up and sputtered. "What are you doing?"

"I think I just saved you," I said.

"Oh. Well.. Okay... Thanks then," he said and shook his little wings.

"You're welcome," I said sarcastically.

"Look, I appreciate you saving me or whatever. Don't make it weird," Loftus said.

"You want some cheese? I could use some food," I said.

"Now you're talking," Loftus replied.

Epilogue

"So, he set you up for the murder?" Rook asked the next morning. "Like, he was trying to frame you, drug you, and then put you away?"

"That seems to be it," I said. "I was the new person in town, and he was taking advantage of my arrival. Apparently, new people in a small town are automatically suspect."

"How did he know you were going to become a patient?" Rook asked before taking a bite of the French toast I'd made for our breakfast. He glossed over my comment about small town distrust of new residents.

"He didn't. That was just a lucky break, and probably the reason he was so eager to get me in the same day for an appointment. Looking back, I should have realized that was a red flag. What kind of doctor stays late to give you a same-day appointment?" I asked.

"A small-town doctor," Rook said. "But it doesn't matter now. It's over. I'm just glad you're okay."

I smiled at him. There was that undercurrent in his voice again when he said he was glad I was okay. Some sort of emotion I couldn't quite place, but I had a plate full of French toast in front of me. I decided to focus on that.

"Me too," I said. "It's good to be home."

Even as I said the words, and really felt like Fullmourn was my new home, I knew it wasn't over. I could feel it like an electric charge in the air around me.

If George Cadell's ghost had tormented me until I solved his murder, there would be others.

Eventually, they would come.

Thank you for reading!

Made in United States
Orlando, FL
10 May 2022

17715949R00150